LOVE, BY GEORGE
Debra Salonen

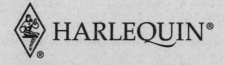

HARLEQUIN®

TORONTO • NEW YORK • LONDON
AMSTERDAM • PARIS • SYDNEY • HAMBURG
STOCKHOLM • ATHENS • TOKYO • MILAN • MADRID
PRAGUE • WARSAW • BUDAPEST • AUCKLAND

ISBN-13: 978-0-373-71434-6
ISBN-10:   0-373-71434-3

LOVE, BY GEORGE

www.eHarlequin.com

Printed in U.S.A.

Kara hadn't seen Brad in years

But he looked the same. Tall. Lean. Broad shoulders that seemed unnaturally tense at the moment. She'd known him since she was seventeen. If anyone had asked her, she'd have said he was a nice guy, a good boss and a so-so pet owner.

Then why this silly breathlessness? Just because he was handsome? Couldn't be. She didn't have time for men.

"Kara. I'm really sorry for this."

"No problem. George must have rolled in something dead on his way here, so we went ahead and bathed him." She leaned over to undo the complicated restraint and was rewarded with a big, wet doggy kiss on the cheek. "Not now, George. Your dad is watching."

Brad burst out laughing, which caused George to turn his head sharply. His snout caught Kara across the nose and she saw stars.

Brad put his hand on her elbow. "You okay?"

She took a deep breath. "Fine."

He let go and backed away. "I...um...kennel up, George." He motioned for the dog to get into the back of the truck.

George looked at Kara like a kid asking, "Do I have to?"

She repressed a smile. "George, as I tell my daughters, you have to take responsibility for your actions. Time to pay the piper, big boy."

Dear Reader,

Show of hands—who loves dogs?

George, one of the main characters in this book, is a dog. A smart, silly, funny, kind-hearted soul in a dog's body. He's also a product of a broken home, and one day he sets out to find the piece that's missing from his previously very nice life. George needs a woman. Someone who will remember to feed him on time; someone to pet him and tell him he's wonderful. And he has just the woman in mind—Kara. His dog groomer.

Kara Williams is a busy, single mother of five-year-old twins. She also owns a pet-grooming business and has big dreams where that's concerned. She's not in the market for a dog, nor is she looking for love. But when George shows up at the Paws Spa one afternoon—she can't turn him away. Truth is she likes George. And before long, she discovers she feels the same about his owner, Brad Ralston.

Brad, George's owner by default after his wife left him, is struggling to keep his life together. For a single father with a demanding business, a runaway dog is a problem. But George is a Great Dane, which makes him a very large problem—until a hug from Kara has Brad wondering if maybe his dog is the smartest one of all.

For those of you who are curious about what was going through George's mind as the story was unfolding, you'll find a preface to each chapter in George's point of view on my Web site at www.debrasalonen.com.

And lest I run the risk of alienating cat lovers, let me add that *Love, By George* has four resident felines, as well. And one very outspoken cat enthusiast by the name of Wilma.

Happy reading!

Debra

ABOUT THE AUTHOR

As a child, Debra Salonen wanted to be an artist. She saved her allowance to send away for a "Learn To Draw" kit, but when her mother mistook Deb's artful rendition of a horse for a cow, Deb turned to her second love—writing. She credits her success as an author to her parents for giving her the chance to realize those dreams. She and her high school sweetheart, who have been married for over thirty years, live in California surrounded by a great deal of family, quite a few dogs and views that appeal to the artist still trapped in her soul.

Books by Debra Salonen

HARLEQUIN SUPERROMANCE

1003–SOMETHING ABOUT EVE
1061–WONDERS NEVER CEASE
1098–MY HUSBAND, MY BABIES
1104–WITHOUT A PAST
1110–THE COMEBACK GIRL
1196–A COWBOY SUMMER
1238–CALEB'S CHRISTMAS WISH
1279–HIS REAL FATHER
1386–A BABY ON THE WAY

SIGNATURE SELECT SAGA

BETTING ON GRACE

HARLEQUIN AMERICAN ROMANCE

1114–ONE DADDY TOO MANY
1126–BRINGING BABY HOME
1139–THE QUIET CHILD

For Paul, my rock and best friend

CHAPTER ONE

"OH, GEORGE, WHAT HAVE YOU done? Are you trying to get me arrested for dognapping?"

The six-year-old Harlequin Great Dane dropped to a crouch, his gaze not meeting hers. Kara Williams's heart just about broke in half. She loved animals, and this big galoot was one of her favorite clients at The Paws Spa, her Pine Harbor, Oregon, pet-grooming business. He'd been one of her regulars until his owners, Brad and Lynette Ralston, split up. Now, Brad, who had custody of George and the couple's teenage son, routinely missed George's standing appointment.

Kara poked her head out the door to check the parking lot. Nope. No Brad. But she'd already figured that out after hearing George's loud woof and no sound of a car pulling in. Apparently George had decided to keep the appointment himself. Even if this was the wrong time and the wrong day.

Glancing at his big muddy paws, she guessed that his escape from the Ralstons' backyard had included some kind of digging. Sticks and weeds had attached themselves to his smooth black and white coat, and there was a bit of blood on his right ear. "Poor guy. This wasn't easy for you, was it?"

She went down on one knee and hugged the silly beast. She'd witnessed the aftermath of divorce—in dog terms—too many times. And it was never pleasant. Some animals would worry an open wound to the point where they had to wear a protective collar. Certain cats she'd met had suddenly turned into domestic demons that shredded curtains and left stinky deposits in their owners' shoes.

"Maybe I should be thankful Fly took off before he had a chance to put a ring on my finger," she murmured, gently stroking the big dog's powerful neck.

Fly had been her youthful folly. Her walk on the wild side. A walk that had resulted in twins.

"Come on in, boy," she said, opening the door of what had formerly been a 1960s era Laundromat. When she returned home halfway through her sophomore year of college to help care for her uncle Kurt, who'd been like a father to her, she'd found a job as a part-time dog groomer—and had fallen in love with the business. When the owner decided to retire and move out of the area, Kurt had encouraged Kara to open her own place—one she could put her unique stamp on.

The Paws Spa had just celebrated its seventh anniversary, and so much had happened in her life since that initial ribbon cutting. Meeting Fly (whose real name was Phil), getting pregnant, becoming a single mom to twins, losing Uncle Kurt. Her life had changed in so many ways, but the one constant was her commitment to her clients—and her dream.

"Watch your tail," she warned as George stepped through the doorway.

The sounds and smells that were so familiar to her enveloped them both as she followed George into the entry. The building was a rectangular block-walled edifice with four skylights and four plate-glass windows that faced the parking lot. When she and Uncle Kurt had first looked at it, it had been gutted, except for two rows of pipes sticking up where the washing machines had been. He'd been in remission at the time, and had provided the financial backing and the expertise to help her remodel.

It wasn't ideal but it served her needs. Half of the area was devoted to grooming stations and holding pens. The entry was spacious enough to provide owners a chance to peruse current animal magazines or shop for special extras for their pets. In the far corner was her tiny office.

"Who have you got there?" her friend and assistant Wilma Donning asked. "Why, George Ralston, does your father know you're here?"

George dipped his head in a way that made him look so guilt-ridden, both women burst out laughing. Kara and Wilma had a tendency to talk to all the pets in their care as if the animals understood every word. A select few responded with gestures and mannerisms that made Kara think they were reacting to her words, not her tone. George was one of those expressive types. Maybe it was his eyes—one blue, one brown. There was humor, intelligence, compassion and trust in those eyes.

"Let's not worry about how he got here," Kara said, grabbing a lead from the hook by the door. "He's pretty stinky, and since Mrs. Fox canceled we have an opening. I'll call Mr. Ralston and let him know George is safe."

"As if he cares," Wilma grumbled. "Darned people who let their crazy love lives affect their animals' welfare."

Wilma was eighty-something. The exact number seemed to depend upon whom she was trying to impress or what point she was trying to make. But she was as feisty and energetic as some people half her age. She didn't have to work—Wilma and her husband had owned one of the biggest organic farming operations in the Pine Harbor area for as long as Kara could remember, and she'd sold it for a healthy sum after he passed away. Now she worked for Kara because, as Wilma often said, "Animals have humans beat, paws down."

Kara once asked why Wilma hadn't chosen to volunteer at the SPCA since she loved animals so much. "Don't care for the bureaucracy," Wilma had returned.

So the SPCA's loss was Kara's gain. Wilma could come off a bit gruff and abrupt with people, but the animals loved her. And Wilma also kept Kara grounded where her dreams were concerned.

Kara planned to turn The Paws Spa into a nationally franchised operation—like the Starbucks of pet grooming. High end. Catering to pet owners who wanted the very best for their animals—specialty grooming for show dogs, organic snacks, massage, yoga classes and group play dates.

The Pine Harbor Paws Spa was her prototype, but already her books were running in the black. Kara recorded every success and failure in a log that she hoped to use as a blueprint for future franchises.

Wilma was as dedicated an employee as Kara could ever have wished for. She came in early and stayed late. She even picked up or delivered animals for clients who were behind schedule. Kara longed for the day when she could pay Wilma what she was worth—even though the older woman insisted she was happy with the way things were.

"More business means more owners to deal with," she'd complain whenever Kara waxed enthusiastic about some new idea to increase her business.

But just as the animals in Wilma's care sensed how much the older woman loved them, Kara knew that deep down Wilma wanted her to succeed. She watched the tiny woman walk the huge dog to the bathing area that had been set up for large animals. George could have knocked Wilma over with his tail, but he was extremely courteous and careful around her.

Kara's heart did a familiar flip-flop and tears welled up in her eyes. Sometimes she thought her sappy emotions were the source of all her problems. "You're an old softy," her uncle used to say. "Just like your dad."

Kara didn't remember much about her father, who'd died when she was eight. His twin brother, Kurt, had been a substitute dad for most of her life. But he was gone now, too. And she still missed him. His parting gift to her had been the deed to this building, and Kara was determined to make him proud of her.

Returning her focus to the present, she walked to her desk for the phone. She quickly checked her client list, found the number for Willowby's, the upscale restaurant that Brad Ralston owned, and then turned to the large box that had been delivered that morning. An expert multitasker—as any mother of twins needed to be—she slipped the microphone attachment over her ear, pocketed the phone and started unpacking the new line of specialty collars and leashes she'd ordered.

As an avid student of millionaire entrepreneurs-cum-authors Robert Kiyosaki and Donald Trump, Kara knew she needed to be focused, more business-minded and fearless in the face of risk if she wanted to make her dream a reality. Successful franchises didn't just appear. They took work, dedication and determination.

"You've reached Willowby's," came the smooth, throaty tone of a woman's voice that Kara remembered all too well. Brad hadn't changed the message on his answering machine after his wife left?

"Funny," she mumbled.

"To make a reservation—" Kara hung up.

She hadn't eaten at the place in years. Not since Kurt had taken her and her mother to brunch there when she was pregnant with the twins. Prior to that, the last time had been when she was a waitress. Staff had been allowed to eat at a discounted price, but often Brad would give leftovers to his servers after the kitchen had closed for the night. Brad Ralston had been a decent guy to work for, Kara remembered. She'd never had the same fondness for his wife, who had served as hostess and oversaw the hiring and firing of employees. Since Kara had been too young to drink, she'd rarely crossed paths with Reggie something or other, Brad's partner who used to run Willowby's bar.

"He's not picking up at the restaurant," she told Wilma, who was scrubbing George with such vigor the dog looked ready to melt into a puddle of bliss. "I'll try his house. I don't think we have his cell number." She returned to her desk and consulted the client card. "Nope. Just Lynette's." *But there's a line through it.*

She didn't remember doing that, but she probably had. Everyone in town had heard about Lynette's running off with Reggie.

She punched in the home number. Another answering machine. Brad's voice this time. She'd always liked his voice. As she waited for the beep, she wondered how true the rumors and scandal surrounding the Ralstons' divorce had been. Some said the two lovers had embezzled from the business before leaving town.

"Um, hi, um, Brad…er, Mr. Ralston. This is Kara Williams calling from The Paws Spa. I just wanted to let you know that George showed up today. By himself. I don't know exactly how or why, but since he…um…you…um…missed his last appointment, I'm going to go ahead and bathe him and trim his nails. He'll be fine here until you show up to get him. Thanks." She almost hung up then remembered she needed to leave her number. She felt her cheeks flush with embarrassment. That was the silliest, most unprofessional message she'd ever left.

"What is wrong with me?"

She knew the answer, but she didn't want to acknowledge it. "I do not still have a crush on Brad Ralston. I was a dumb kid back then and he was a married man. I wanted something I couldn't have. I'm soooo over that kind of adolescent thrill-seeking behavior," she said with verve.

"Are you talking to yourself again?" Wilma called over the sound of water spraying.

"No. Just leaving a message. He didn't answer at either number."

"Probably had to go to the school to pick up his kid," Wilma said.

"Why do you say that?" Kara asked as she walked

to the comfortably appointed wire kennels where two dogs in separate holding pens were having a discussion of their own. She gave each animal a treat from her pocket. "Good boy, Hunter. Your mom will be here soon." A mixed breed with beagle ears and an excitable personality, Hunter took her offering and paced around, no doubt looking for a spot to bury it.

"Here you go, Pansy. Chew your bone like a good girl." Pansy, a cocker spaniel, was twelve, overweight and highly pampered.

Kara turned her attention back to Wilma. "What were you saying about Brad's son?"

"Margaret Mieda in my bridge group. Her daughter drives a school bus. She says Brad's boy has got a real attitude problem."

Kara removed her earphone and dropped the unit on her desk, pausing to pet Whitey and Tiger, her two resident "guard" cats. The neutered males usually ducked out of sight when large dogs appeared, but they'd never seemed intimidated by George, and with Pansy and Hunter safely behind bars, they obviously felt brave enough to nap on her keyboard.

"That's too bad. Maybe that explains why George has missed so many appointments."

Wilma's bridge group met every Tuesday morning, and she always returned to work with an earful of gossip. "It's not surprising that the boy has problems. Dogs aren't the only ones that take it to heart when a family falls apart."

Kara agreed. That was partly why she planned not to get involved seriously with any man until after her children were through school. Maybe even college. Why take the risk? Her mother's impulsive marriage to a man who promised to take care of her and her little girl but wound up doing just the opposite had shaped Kara's opinion of matrimony for the worse. And her own experience with Fly had confirmed that love was like stepping off the edge of the world. The free fall might be exciting, but the landing hurt like hell.

BRAD TIGHTENED HIS HANDS around the padded steering wheel cover. This was the third time this month he'd been called to the Pine Harbor Junior High because his son was in trouble. First, Justin had been caught smoking in the locker room, which had resulted in him getting kicked off the soccer team. Next, he'd been accused of instigating a food fight in the cafeteria. So now Brad packed his lunch the night before. This morning, it seemed some younger schoolmates overheard Justin using bad language on the bus.

Nothing so dire that his son faced expulsion, but every little annoying incident meant Brad had to leave the restaurant, which was on the coast, about five miles from central Pine Harbor, drive back into town and deal with the serious, disapproving looks that seemed quick to judge his parenting skills—or lack of them.

Brad had tried to explain that Justin was four-teen—and going through a rough time, but that excuse was growing thin. He was every bit as frus-trated as Justin's teachers and bus driver must be, but what was he supposed to do? An initial show of patience, later followed by grounding and lectures hadn't done the trick. Nothing he said seemed to faze Justin in the least.

Which, if he thought about it, wasn't surprising. With Justin's mother gone, the only functional line of communication between father and son had disappeared. Brad blamed himself—and Lynette. She could have done more to foster a relationship between father and son, but that would have under-mined her role—that of indispensable, all-control-ling wife, mother, businesswoman.

At the school, Brad and Justin met with Mrs. La Rue, the principal, for about twenty minutes, and then she sent Justin to the bus building to pick up a formal warning and notice of two weeks' suspension from the bus. The passenger door of the Tahoe opened and Justin got in. The loud slam echoed in the huge SUV, reminding Brad that he'd planned to sell the gas hog. With Lynette gone, there was no need for such a big vehicle. No sports meant no more car pooling. And Brad's schedule didn't allow for driving and dropping off neighbors' kids and friends every morning and afternoon, which meant Justin had to ride the bus. At least that had been the case until today.

"Did you get the letter?"

Justin grunted and reached for the radio controls.

Brad blocked his hand. "Not yet. We need to talk. If you can't ride the bus, then you're going to have to get up half an hour earlier to walk to school."

"Walk?" Justin shouted. "Are you out of your freakin' mind? Only losers walk."

"Losers and people who are kicked off the bus. What did you think would happen? That everybody would give you a break because you think you have a right to that chip on your shoulder?"

Justin's green eyes—identical to his mother's—narrowed to a look designed to show exactly how much he hated everyone, especially Brad. "Whatever."

Brad stifled a sigh. He hated that word. It made him want to punch something. But never some*one.* He wasn't the violent type.

"Hit me, man. Get it over with and just do it. We both know I deserve it," his best friend and partner, Reggie Crenshaw, had begged him a little over a year ago. Right after the audit, but before Brad had found out about the affair.

"Just tell me why?" Brad had asked, too numb with shock to fully comprehend the extent of the betrayal. "And how?" he'd added, mind-boggled by the numbers the auditor had been tossing around.

The answers were linked, of course. Both questions led to Lynette. Her frequent trips to church retreats, women's empowerment groups and business seminars had turned out to be romantic trysts, usually at a casino since gambling was Reggie's admitted vice, completely paid for by Willowby's.

Only now did Brad regret not beating the crap out of his friend when he'd had the chance. His left hand gripped the steering wheel as he put the truck in gear. Violence wasn't the answer. Work was.

"I'm taking you to the restaurant. You can do your homework in my office then do dishes."

"No way. I wanna go home."

"Tough. I'm running late with setup because of this."

"What about George?"

"What about him?"

"I thought I was supposed to walk him after school."

Damn. George was Brad's *other* problem child. Only, he was a four-legged one. "A boy needs a dog," Lynette had claimed. "You're so busy with work Justin is lonely," she'd added, twisting the guilt knife a little deeper in his ribs.

So she'd searched online until she found a breeder who sold them a registered Harlequin Great Dane puppy. White with black spots, Brad's first thought had been they'd gotten a Dalmatian by mistake— until he saw the size of George's paws.

"Fine. We'll pick him up and you can walk him on the beach before you do your homework."

Justin let out a groan and slumped in his seat. His little iPod earphones went into his ears and some disparate beat that Brad refused to call music resonated softly in the car.

Premature deafness. One more worry on Brad's plate. But it was one of so many he really couldn't give it much attention. His mind was already racing ahead to what kind of drama the night would bring. He thought of his restaurant as a kind of theater, where every evening he was the director, bringing together high art, delicious food and understated elegance on center stage, with madness and mayhem just behind the curtain.

He was still debating about whether to make a garlic chipotle sauce or something lighter to serve with the fresh tilapia that had been delivered that morning when they pulled into the driveway of the 1980s one-story ranch house he and Lynette bought as newlyweds. His father's unexpected death and generous bequeathal had provided enough extra cash to purchase the empty two-point-five acre lot next to them a few years later. That lot was presently standing in the way of the closure of their property settlement.

"Go get George. And don't forget his leash," Brad said, nudging his son's elbow.

"Don't push me," Justin cried, pulling back.

Brad groaned softly. He honestly didn't know what to do anymore. The little kid who once loved to work by his side in the kitchen now couldn't stand to be in the same room—the same house—with him. Most of the time, Justin hid out in the addition Lynette had had built six or so years earlier.

"My family needs a place to stay when they come. It will add to our home's value and someday when we're old and gray, Justin and his wife can have the main house and they'll take care of us in the addition," she'd argued.

"Right," Brad muttered now, glancing at his watch.

He was just starting to open the door when Justin returned, carrying George's leash. There was no dog in sight—and a dog of George's size was hard to miss. In his left hand was the portable phone.

Brad rolled down the window. "Where's George?"

"Here," his son said, handing him the phone.

Brad pushed a button to replay the message. He didn't recognize the voice at first, but it only took a few seconds to put a face to the name the speaker gave. Kara Williams. Lithesome blond beauty who once worked for him at the restaurant but was now the owner of a dog-grooming service Lynette had insisted they bring George to.

"Damn," he swore. "You were supposed to make sure George was in his pen before you went to school."

Justin's anger was unmistakable. "I knew you'd blame me. You blame me for everything that goes wrong around here. Screw it. I'm not going with you and you can't make me."

He stormed off into the house, slamming the door behind him.

Brad turned off the phone. He got out of the truck and walked around the side of the garage to the chain-link fence of the dog run. A large, sturdy doghouse made with the same wood siding as the house was set in one corner, under the overhang. Dog toys and a child's plastic swimming pool gave the place a cheerful look. A fresh mound of dirt surrounding a natural indentation where water drained away from the house told him what had happened. His giant dog had turned into a giant gopher.

He leaned his head against the six-foot fence. The metal was cool and soothing, but the chill wasn't enough to block the pain throbbing in his skull. His life was turning into a big black hole and his dog was digging it deeper. He couldn't get rid of his restaurant or his house or his son, but he could do something about George. He'd ask Kara. She worked with pets and pet owners every day. Maybe she knew of someone who might just have a home for a Great Dane.

CHAPTER TWO

"WELL, BOY, NO CALL from your dad, so it looks like you're going home with me," Kara told the dog who had been tracking her moves the whole time he'd been at the Paws Spa. He peered at her with a semblance of devotion that left her slightly unnerved.

Wilma had left an hour earlier, after their final scheduled client of the day, a Siberian husky named Mush, was picked up. Mush's owners were two professional women who planned to participate in the Iditarod. Someday. They'd purchased Mush to get in the spirit of the challenge. Unfortunately, neither seemed to have the time or inclination to train the poor animal.

Mush was a mess.

George, who possessed a calm disposition and keen intelligence that poor Mush lacked entirely, had cleaned up nicely. His white areas were white again—even his feet. She'd applied a bit of antiseptic to his torn ear and had trimmed his nails, which had taken some extra time, given the mud, but he'd rested in the sun after his bath and had enjoyed a nap and an organic snack while waiting for his master. Who didn't appear to be coming.

She'd tried Brad's house again, but the line had been busy. She glanced at the clock over the door. "We'd better go, boy. Esmeralda doesn't like it when I'm late. She says the girls fret."

Her day-care provider was a gem. A grandmother with eight children scattered around the state, Esmeralda Barejo ran a babysitting service in her home, which was right next door to the tiny house Kara rented. Kara's place was too small and in pretty rough condition, but the convenience and low rent were worth the occasional tussle with cockroaches and ant infestations.

The twins, who would turn six in July, went to kindergarten every morning and were returned by bus to Esmeralda's at noon. Next year they would be in first grade and in school full-time. Kara couldn't wait. The money she'd save on day care would get her closer to her long-term goals.

She was tired of people—mostly her mother— telling her what a long shot her dream was. She'd been a business student in college until Uncle Kurt got sick. She'd helped care for him, driving him to and from doctors' appointments and treatments, because there had been no one else to do it. She'd thought about returning to school after he went into remission, but by then her employer was talking about retiring and the opportunity to take over the business had been too great to resist.

And when she got pregnant with twins, her plans were really thrown off schedule. But she had ambition and she wasn't going to let the daily grind suck her down into a small life that consisted merely of making ends meet.

She was reaching for her keys when the phone rang. Assuming the caller was Brad, she raced to pick it up. "The Paws Spa, Kara speaking."

"Kara, good. You're there. I was hoping to catch you before you left. I need a couple of things from the store. Could you stop for me on your way home?"

"Not really, Mom. I'm waiting for a client to pick up his dog and I need to get the girls. Why? Is something wrong with your car?"

Her mother's overly long pause told Kara the news wasn't going to be good. "It's in police impound. Tony got picked up for driving without a license last night."

Tony was her mother's current live-in boyfriend. For the most part, he was a nice guy. A self-employed handyman-slash-carpenter who had helped Kara after the last big storm blew in the front door at The Paws Spa and soaked a bunch of the wallboard. By far the best of the bunch if Kara reflected on her mother's choices of men. Unfortunately, however, he had a problem with alcohol.

"I had to bail him out of jail and didn't have enough to cover my car, too."

"Maybe you should have chosen the car."

"Don't go all righteous on me, Kara. Tony is

trying. He just slipped. We're not all perfect, you know."

Nancy Barre, or Nan, as she preferred to be called, wasn't dumb or incapable—only a very poor judge of character where men were concerned. She had a decent job working for the phone company and could have been looking forward to a comfortable retirement if not for the money she'd invested in her loser boyfriends.

"Make a list, Mom. The girls and I can drive you to the store after dinner."

Nan didn't reply right away. When she did it was clear she was slightly put out. "Okay. I guess we can get by with canned soup for now."

Kara didn't bother pointing out that if Tony were a grown-up who went to his AA meetings instead of hanging out at bars, they would have food in the cupboard. Just one more reason she was glad Fly was out of her life. "I'll be there as soon as I can, Mom. Gotta run. 'Bye."

She hung up and turned to George, who was watching her intently. His left brow—the one over his blue eye—lifted as if he were asking what was troubling her.

"My mother drives me crazy. I know she's had some bad breaks, like my dad dying, but why does she always pick men who are needy or damaged or—in Doug's case—insane?" She shuddered at the mention of her first stepfather's name. "At least Tony isn't abusive, but she could do so much better. Sometimes I want to scream."

George's expression changed from concern to worry. She leaned down and gave him a hug. "It's okay. You probably have enough tension in your life. I promise to drop you off before the girls and I head over to Mom's."

She slipped a spare lead over his head and picked up her tote bag that contained her purse, Thermos and leftovers from her brown-bag lunch. No takeout for her. Every penny counted when you were a single mom with big aspirations.

"Hop in, my friend," she said, opening the rear door, which sported her logo in pink and brown lettering, bracketed by two George-size paw prints.

She'd just finished securing George with a makeshift seat belt when a SUV roared into the parking lot.

Brad Ralston hopped out, walked to the back of his truck to open one of the doors and then headed her way.

Kara hadn't talked to him in years. On those rare occasions when he'd remembered George's appointment, he'd typically send his son in with a check to settle the bill. But he looked much as she remembered him. Tall. Lean. Broad shoulders that looked unnaturally tense at the moment. His thick dark hair was wind-tossed and needed trimming. He was dressed casually in black jeans, a dark green Polo shirt under a gray fleece pullover sporting the Willowby's logo and athletic shoes.

Her heart sped up as if she were afraid, which she

wasn't. She'd known him since she was seventeen. If anyone would have asked her, she'd have told them he was a nice guy, a good boss and a so-so pet owner. Before the Ralstons split up, Lynette had handled George's appointments. She'd complained that Brad wasn't into owning a dog, but he paid the bill in a timely manner and that was all that mattered to Kara. Right?

Then why this silly breathlessness? Just because he was as handsome as she remembered? No. Couldn't be. She didn't have time for men.

"Kara. I'm glad I caught you. I just got home and heard your message. I tried calling from the road but your line was busy. I'm really sorry for this."

"No problem. I just didn't want you to worry about him. It was pretty obvious he dug his way free. And he was awful smelly—Wilma thinks he must have rolled in something dead on his way here—so, we went ahead and bathed him," she said, leaning over to undo the complicated restraint she'd just tied.

She didn't want to imagine what kind of picture she presented—butt sticking out, grubby jeans, over-sized sweatshirt that would have displayed even more if she hadn't worn several layers beneath it.

"That's good. I'm sure he needed grooming. I know we've missed a couple of appointments. So much to do…I don't have the routine down yet."

"I understand, but I should warn you. I've been toying with the idea of charging a missed appointment fee. I know you can appreciate how frustrating it is to hold a reservation—turning away other business—and not having the party show up. It's a little different in the restaurant business since you can fill that table with drop-ins, but…"

"You're right. You shouldn't be penalized for my incompetence. Let me pay you for the dates I missed."

She turned sideways to look at him. He'd always been decisive and fair in her waitress days, but now his tone seemed too resigned.

"Hey, this is dog grooming, not brain surgery. I can guarantee you're the only client who would be this agreeable about getting charged for a service that wasn't rendered. I appreciate your offer, but I'm not adding anything to your bill this time, but I'd just prefer it if you'd call if you can't make George's standing appointments in the future."

She returned to her efforts and was rewarded with a big, wet doggy lick on her cheek. She scrunched up her face. "Not now, George. Your dad is watching."

Brad burst out laughing, which caused George to turn his head sharply. His snout struck Kara across the nose and she momentarily saw spots. She somehow managed to undo the last knot and backed out of the car, still a little dizzy.

A hand on her elbow alerted her to Brad's nearness. "You okay?"

She took a deep breath. "Fine. Stood up too fast."

He let go and backed up, but not before she

inhaled his scent. Herbs and garlic. Willowby's before the rush. One of her favorite memories.

"I…um…kennel up, George," he said, motioning with his arm for the dog to get into the back of the truck.

George looked at Kara like a kid asking, "Do I have to?"

She repressed a smile. "George, as I tell my daughters, you have to take responsibility for your actions. Time to pay the piper, big boy."

He sighed heavily and trudged across the parking lot. His long legs made climbing into the open area behind the rear seat a snap. He turned around twice then finally sat down, peering around the half-open door.

Brad hesitated as if searching for something to say. In the distance, Kara could hear the phone in The Paws Spa ringing. Brad's left brow tilted diagonally—just like George's.

"Either my sitter or my mom," she said by way of an explanation. "I've gotta dash. Thanks for picking him up. My girls would have tried to adopt him if I took him home with me, and if you could see my house, you'd know why that wouldn't be a good idea."

She closed the rear door and started to get in her car, but paused when Brad said, "Thanks, Kara. Some days I think just one more straw really will do me in. Today it was George. It's too bad you're not in the market for a Great Dane. I think he prefers you over me."

Her heart melted at his defeatist tone. She'd been down that road herself after Fly left. She'd rallied and so would he. She just hoped he wouldn't do something he'd regret, like getting rid of his son's dog. Impulsively, she walked to where he was standing, put her arms around him and squeezed tightly. "Don't give up. On yourself or George. Things will get better. I promise."

Then, feeling about as ridiculous as possible, she hurried back to her car and pulled away. Nuts. He must think she was completely, utterly nuts.

BRAD DROVE HOME in silence and relative peace. No panicky calls on his cell phone, thank goodness. Only George's piglike snore coming from the far back. He thought about taking the dog with him to work, but he knew from experience how dangerous that was unless Justin was around.

Instead, he detoured through town, at the height of rush hour. Not that traffic in Pine Harbor rivaled that of any big city, but the area was growing and the infrastructure hadn't kept up. As he waited at a stop-light, he thought about Kara.

Kara Williams. He could still remember her first day as a waitress. Lynette had hired Kara and two other high school students to work weekends. All three would start as water girls and work their way up to taking orders. Of the three, only Kara stuck it out.

By the time she left to go away to college, she was

their top waitress. Brad had missed her perky attitude and work ethic—very few people her age had the ability to see a need and fill it without being told how and why—but he had been happy to see her pursue an education. He'd been surprised and saddened when someone told him she had to drop out of school to care for her uncle. He hadn't crossed paths with her much, but he'd seen her once on the beach with a guy with a ponytail and a tattoo.

Like in any small town, people talked. He heard she was working as a dog groomer, and eventually someone mentioned the birth of her twins. "Poor Kara," he'd overheard Lynette telling someone. "The girl had such potential, but she wasted it on the wrong man and now she's stuck in Pine Harbor."

But tonight, she'd been the one consoling him. And her hug had helped. A lot.

The light changed and he stepped on the gas. A bit too heavily. The big truck lunged forward. George let out a small yelp.

"Sorry, George. I forgot about you." Again. His guilty conscience was getting quite a workout.

"Justin will feed you when we get home, buddy. He's grounded for life, so the only time he gets out of the house is to go to school and to walk you. This is a good thing for you, Georgie-boy."

Hearing the silly nickname Lynette had used when talking to the dog, George sat up. She'd also used baby talk that had made Brad want to scream. Not that he ever did. Nope, good ol' easygoing Brad.

A hard-ass in the kitchen, but a pushover in the rest of his life.

Don't give up. Things will get better.

How did Kara know that? And when? he wanted to ask. After his son left home or got thrown in jail? After Brad was forced to declare bankruptcy because he couldn't afford to pay taxes on all the money his ex-wife and ex-partner had siphoned off the books?

Maybe things would improve if he downsized, simplified. He could start by selling the house. His mother had advised not doing anything drastic when she'd been here for the holidays, but he and Justin didn't need such a big place. And, despite what Kara said, he would put out some feelers about finding a new home for George. *I don't have enough time to be a diligent, responsible dog owner.*

The word responsible brought back to mind Kara's gentle lecture to George. If she was teaching her little girls—who surely couldn't be more than four or five—to live up to their actions, then he could do the same with his son.

Ten minutes later, he pulled into the driveway, got out and opened the rear door for George.

The dog exited with a dignity that Brad found rather endearing. He liked George; he simply didn't have the energy it took to boss Justin into caring for the dog.

But until he found George another home, Brad was going to do just that. And his grouchy, unhappy son wasn't going to like the arrangement one bit.

Oh, well.

CHAPTER THREE

BRAD OPENED HIS EYES and stared into the blackness.

He'd woken up early to make sure Justin left for school on time. His son had made it clear he resented the fact that Brad wouldn't get dressed and drive him to school. They'd had the same argument every morning for a week. The bitter sniping made it impossible for Brad to go back to sleep after Justin left, so this morning he hadn't even gotten out of bed. Instead, he'd tried to listen closely to his son's routine, picturing him as he ate cereal, talked to someone on the phone and did his few chores. Brad hoped Justin had remembered to feed George. By the persistent complaining sounds George was making Brad couldn't be sure.

In the past, Brad had been able to sleep until ten every day. Since his night shift usually ended at one or two a.m., depending on how long it took to clean the grills and wind down from the rush, he'd felt entitled. Lynette had been responsible for getting Justin off to school—a role that she'd embraced with such fervor she wound up taxiing four or five other kids to school every day, in addition to Justin. Brad had slept through every chaotic moment.

Now, he rushed home as early as possible on the weeknights that Justin was home alone. His son was a pretty responsible fourteen-year-old, and Brad usually talked to him a couple of times each evening to make sure everything was okay, but Brad wasn't happy with the arrangement. He thanked God they lived at the end of a cul-de-sac. He knew his vigilant neighbors would call if a carload of kids showed up to party.

He blamed Lynette for the fact their son was home alone. They'd had a perfect division of duties until the day she told him she was having an affair with his partner—the man Brad believed had been cooking the books of their business for years. Brad had expected Lynette to share his outrage when he'd voiced his suspicions. Instead, she'd admitted her own culpability.

The only reason she and Reggie weren't in jail was the deal they'd cut with the D.A. A deal Brad had supported. They were paying him back, slowly but surely. The money barely made a drop in his bucket of legal fees, but it helped assuage a tiny bit of the blow to his ego.

But his accountant was still negotiating with the IRS, and no one knew what the total bill might run. Plus, the money did nothing to stem the pain from Lynette's defection. She'd left the country with Reggie for some exotic paradise while he was stuck here trying to maintain a dream he no longer recognized—or was sure he wanted.

Lynette called Justin weekly, but ever since Christmas when her gift to her son arrived ten days late, Justin seemed to be avoiding her calls. When they did talk—from what Brad occasionally overheard—the conversations were stiff and awkward. Justin's side usually consisted of grunts and "uh-huhs."

His ex-wife's virtual abandonment of their son was the most baffling—and hurtful—aspect of their divorce, as far as Brad was concerned. She hadn't been back to see him in six months. She hadn't made any plans for him to visit her over the holidays or spring break.

"No wonder the kid is messed up," he said aloud, his stomach making a sound not unlike George's grumblings.

Brad wondered if Justin had fed the poor animal before leaving for school. He hadn't seen any signs of a dog food can sitting on the counter last night when he'd come home. With a resigned sigh, he crawled out of bed and groped for the bedside lamp. The room-darkening shades were the best on the market. Lynette never did anything halfway—even when it came to screwing up his life.

He pulled on a pair of sweats and, after a search in his huge, half-empty walk-in closet, managed to find matching slippers. A gift from some Christmas past.

Christmas. He wasn't sure how they'd survived this past holiday season. His mother's presence had helped, but she'd returned to her Arizona retirement community in time for a big New Year's Eve celebration. Mostly, Brad had worked. He'd tried to stay connected with Justin by putting him to work at the restaurant, but in hindsight he wondered whether he'd chosen the best course.

Maybe I should have closed up and taken Justin to Hawaii or something, he thought, groping his way along the shadowy hall. Made new memories.

But what would we have done with George?

Besides, he told himself, the restaurant was more than just his livelihood—it was his refuge. And his son needed to learn what happened when you let your guard down.

"Never again," he muttered, walking into the kitchen. He could access George's pen by way of the garage. If his food dish was empty, he'd have to come back inside to fill it. They'd had to start keeping the sacks of kibble, which supplemented the dog's canned meat ration, in the house because of raccoons.

Brad stubbed his toe twice, but finally managed to maneuver through the clutter in the garage. Cleaning the garage—a good, after-school job for Justin, he decided. He opened the door and looked out.

The dog run was just a few feet away. George was lying on the far side, facing the street. His food dish appeared to be full, but the water dish was nearly empty. He started to curse under his breath but stopped.

He'd been a teenager once, too. He could remem-

ber his father castigating him for doing only the bare
minimum where his household chores were concerned. "You need to look at the whole picture, Brad-
ley," his father had said in his stern, judgmental
voice. "You'll never get ahead by merely doing what
you're told."

With a sigh, Brad walked to the pen and opened
the latch. George swung his big head around in
obvious surprise and scrambled to his feet, his tail
swishing from side to side. The look on his face said,
"Walk?"

"Sorry, boy," Brad said, carrying the bowl to the
water spigot a few feet away. "Not this morning.
That's Justin's job. He promised to take you right
after school."

The tail stopped swishing.

Brad didn't blame him. Justin's idea of a walk and
George's were probably very different. Feeling an
extra dose of guilt, Brad set the water bowl in place.
His father had been adamant about keeping animals
in their place—outside and out of sight. Brad hadn't
subscribed completely to that school of thought, but
he had never treated George as more than just a pet,
either.

He rubbed the base of George's ear as he'd seen
Kara do. The dog closed his eyes, leaning in to the
touch. If he'd been a cat he would have been purring.
Brad smiled. He could have used a little sensual satisfaction in his life. Too bad that wasn't going to
happen. His divorce had left him an emotional am-

putee. No woman in her right mind would get involved with him—although a few had hinted that they might like to try.

He wasn't interested. His life was already too complicated without adding a relationship to the mix. Even though just petting George brought a certain female dog groomer to mind. A woman who gave great hugs.

If there were a way to have the hugs without the emotional turmoil… He pushed the thought aside. Nope. Wasn't possible.

He rubbed George's broad head and told him, "All women have strings attached, George. Don't you forget that."

George tilted his head quizzically.

Brad turned away and started out of the pen. He paused to add, "I promise to try to remember to make your next appointment, but one thing you gotta know, buddy, Kara's got even more strings than most women. Twins."

George's odd colored eyes opened wide, giving him a shocked look. Brad smiled at his expression. "See you later, George. I have to get ready for wor—" The sound of the phone ringing cut into his thoughts. Dread blossomed in his chest. Phone calls this early usually meant trouble.

He kicked the gate closed on his way out, only half listening for the sound of it connecting. Did it hook? He was sure it had. Pretty sure, anyway.

He ran inside, sliding on the tile floor as he rounded the corner. "Hello?"

His assistant chef. The produce guy was late. Truck problems. Again.

Brad shook his head and sighed. "I'll be there in half an hour. Start calling around and see if you can find another supplier. I'm really sick of their excuses. Why can't people just do their jobs?"

Lately, that refrain had been his mantra. Lynette's job had been to live up to her vows. Reggie's had been to tend bar and keep the books. Accurately. Honestly. And to be a friend. Brad had tried to do his part as he understood it—run Willowby's, serve the kind of food that kept his patrons coming back and make enough money to keep his family happy. But he'd failed. He just wished he knew how.

BANJO, PATTI METZ'S four-year-old boxer, was barking excitedly and jumping around the fenced side yard with a joyful abandon typical of his breed when provoked. And, Kara had to admit, her twins were rambunctious enough to provoke all kinds of behavior. The barking, though, she could definitely live without.

"Banjo. Stop." The word came out with enough force to catch every animal on the property's attention. Even the cats stopped what they were doing.

"Mommy, he likes it."

"We're playing tag."

Sophie and Sadie were fraternal not identical twins, but most people couldn't tell them apart. Even their voices were the same, but Kara knew that

Sophie usually spoke first, with Sadie adding her two cents after her sister.

Kara snapped her fingers and motioned for Banjo to come to her. With a quick click, she had the dog's lead attached to the fancy new collar Patti had bought for him that morning. She praised him for behaving so well, then led the way to the large-breed carrier sitting in the shade of the overhang.

Sophie put her hands on her hips and glared at her mother. Sadie obviously wasn't sure whether to complain or apologize for something.

After closing Banjo in his carrier, Kara walked to them and went down on one knee. "I love it that you want to help. Since Esmeralda had a doctor's appointment this afternoon, you're going to have lots of time to do just that. And exercising the dogs is one way that you can earn some extra money. Unfortunately, Banjo's mother likes him to come home nice and clean after his bath, not dirty and stinky."

"Can they play before their baths?" Sophie asked.

"Yes, but our next client isn't due for half an hour, so in the meantime you could clean the brushes."

Sophie's perky nose scrunched up daintily. "Eeoouu."

The two looked at each other, as if conferring silently, but before Sophie could announce their mutual decision, Sadie let out an excited yip and pointed toward the street. "What about that dog? Can we play with him?"

What dog? Kara hadn't heard a car turn into the parking lot. She glanced over her shoulder.

"Oh, no," she groaned, jumping to her feet. The twins raced to the fence and called for the dog.

George pranced along the sidewalk, seemingly without a care in the world—certainly without a leash or owner in evidence. He let out a happy bark when he spotted them and started loping across the road.

"No, George. Stay." Burney Avenue wasn't a terribly busy thoroughfare, but there were enough cars around to make Kara nervous. The dog kept coming. "At least look both ways."

He didn't.

The sound of brakes screeching made her rush out of the gated yard, motioning for her daughters to wait where there were. They didn't. She ran to the curb, her breath burning in her throat as she anticipated the worst.

The driver of the car flipped her off as he roared away. George, who appeared uninjured, completed his passage, impervious to his near miss or Kara's panic. He trotted right to her side, his tail wagging in greeting, teeth exposed in what passed for a Great Dane grin.

"Oh, George, not again. You are so in trouble."

"Is he lost, Mommy?"

"Can we keep him?"

She watched as her fearless daughters embraced the dog that nearly matched them in height and weighed more than both of them put together. George shivered with joy. His delighted expression destroyed Kara's ability to be stern. She sighed and said, "We're going to keep him until his father comes after him. At least he doesn't need a bath this time. He must not have had to dig his way out of his pen."

She wasn't sure what that meant. At their last encounter, Brad had mentioned the possibility of finding a new home for George. Had he done that? Was George lost from some other owner? She hoped not. The poor animal was obviously lonely, and foisting him on a new family wasn't the answer.

What was the answer? She wasn't sure. But she was honest enough to admit that she kinda liked having an excuse to call Brad again.

She made sure the twins were occupied with giving George water and treats, then she went inside. Wilma handed her the phone. "There's a storm brewing."

"Pardon?"

"I was just talking to my friend who said there's a big storm coming in. The businesses on the coast have been advised to board up. Thought you should know in case Brad Ralston doesn't answer."

Kara blinked. "Wow. You're always two steps ahead of me. Thanks. I don't suppose you put the restaurant on speed dial, did you?"

Wilma made a face. "You know I don't like technology."

Kara knew. "Just teasing. Keep an eye on the girls while I make this call, okay?"

"My pleasure. And, remember, you have a standing invitation to stay at my house if this storm starts looking ugly. I know how you feel about bad weather, and that house you're living in is a piece of junk."

Wilma was an odd duck, but Kara's truest friend. Which was why Kara was careful not to take advantage. She never asked Wilma to babysit, and she rarely brought the twins to work. Except when she had no choice, like when Esmeralda had a doctor's appointment.

"Thanks. I'll keep that in mind. Hopefully this won't be that bad."

She listened to the sound of the phone ringing on the other end and pictured the restaurant. Two stories, with windows on three sides to afford the optimum ocean view. If Brad was outside putting up protective sheets of plywood—

"Hello."

"Brad? It's Kara Williams. I'm sure you're busy getting ready for the storm and all, but George is back. If you can't find time to pick him up, I could run him home for you."

No muttered epithets for Brad Ralston. Just a silent frustration that emanated through the phone line. "The gate must not have hooked. It's tricky."

Kara didn't say anything.

"I'm really sorry about this, Kara. George and I are going to have to have a long talk about his behavior. In the meantime, if you could take him home I'd really appreciate it. We're battening down the hatches here, so to speak. The worst of the surge is supposed to miss us, but the way the wind is picking up, I'm not taking any chances. I promise to make it up to you with dinner some night."

She knew what he meant—a free meal at his restaurant—but her foolish heart reacted as if he'd invited her out on a date. Her mouth went dry and her fingers tingled as if she couldn't quite feel the phone. "Okay," she managed, her voice sounding ridiculously high-pitched and girlish.

"Just make sure the latch clicks. Otherwise, he'll follow you home. Stupid dog."

As in only a stupid dog would follow *her* home? She knew that wasn't what he meant, but the statement helped her get control of her emotions. "I will. He's outside playing with my girls at the moment. We still have a full schedule this afternoon unless the threat of rain scares people away."

"More than rain, they say," he said ominously. "High winds. Rough sea. Possible flooding."

"Are you sure you don't want me to bring George to you? He might be scared to be left home alone."

"A friend is dropping Justin here after school, and we'll be leaving as soon as the plywood is up. George will be fine until we get there."

He'd replied too fast to have given her question any real consideration, Kara thought, but she didn't argue. She was sure George would be safe and dry, but what if he was terrified? Not everyone liked storms. Some people—and dogs—didn't like to be alone during bad weather.

Some people—and dogs—went a little bit crazy during storms. And Kara was one of them. Her twins had been conceived on just such a night—one of the biggest storms to ever hit the central coast. She'd turned to the handiest set of arms around—Fly's, and her life had never been the same.

She hung up and looked out the window at her canine ward, basking in the dual affection of her daughters. She couldn't regret that night, but she wasn't going into this storm unprepared. After she dropped George off, she and the girls would take Wilma up on her offer. They'd be safe inland at Wilma's hundred-year-old farmhouse. The place had survived the worst Mother Nature had to throw at it and was still standing. Before dropping George off, they'd swing by her place and pick up some provisions: sleeping bags, extra clothes and games.

It paid to be prepared when you had children, and Kara had learned the hard way what happened when you tempted fate.

CHAPTER FOUR

"GEORGE, PLEASE STOP whimpering. Brad said to take you home and that's where I'm taking you. You're his dog. He knows what's best. You'll be fine."

Kara didn't know who she was trying to convince, George or herself.

"But, Mommy, why can't he go to Wilma's with us?"

"Because Wilma's cats would eat him alive."

"Whitey and Tiger like him," Sadie said, expanding on her sister's line of thought. "Maybe Pooka and Dilbert would like him, too."

"Pooka and Dilbert don't like anyone—except Wilma. I want you to promise me you'll stay away from them when we get there." Wilma's two feline friends had been rescued from an abusive owner. They had the run of her remote home and rarely saw guests. Kara didn't trust them one bit.

"Will the bunnies be safe?" Sophie asked.

Kara glanced to her right. The only way to fit the metal hutch into the car had been to turn it sideways.

All four lops were squished together in the two-foot square space, a fuzzy patchwork of color visible in the light from her dash. "As long as they're in their cage, they'll be fine." She hoped.

A gust of wind made the small car quiver. George let out a low moan.

Kara glanced over her shoulder. The huge dog, stuck like a statue between her two little girls, stared straight ahead, a worried expression on his face. "We're almost home, George. I sure hope your dad is there."

He wasn't. Either that or the place had already lost power. Brad's closest neighbor was half a block away, and she thought she could see lights coming from that house, so she had to assume her first guess was right.

She pulled into the wide driveway and parked close to the garage to escape some of the punishing wind. A motion-sensitive light came on. This should have alleviated some of Kara's anxiety, but mostly it served to highlight the angle and strength of the driving rain. She undid her seat belt and turned to look behind her. Her daughters' eyes were as big and round as George's.

"Don't take him, Mommy. He'll get wet," Sophie said, throwing her arms around George's chest dramatically.

"He might catch a cold," Sadie added, reaching across from the other side.

Kara didn't try to alleviate their fears. She agreed with them. Dropping George off—alone—in the middle of a storm felt wrong. Inhumane. She grabbed her phone and checked the call log. Yes. Brad's number was there.

The answering machine picked up.

She let out a small groan. A large, slobbery tongue lapped the side of her cheek. She closed her eyes and sat back. "I can't do it, George. I can't take you with us and I can't abandon you in your pen. What if the road washes out and Brad doesn't make it back tonight?"

She knew for a fact how real that possibility was. The road that led to Willowby's and the adjacent coastal neighborhood was where her father had died trying to rescue a stranded motorist.

She grabbed the flashlight she always carried in her car and pulled up the hood of her slicker. "You girls stay here. I'm going to see if I can find a hidden key somewhere."

Sophie undid her seat belt and launched herself forward. "Me and Sadie can look, too."

"It might be under a rock. Like at our house," her sister chimed in, struggling to get free of her booster seat.

"No," Kara said, using the same tone that stopped dogs and cats in their tracks. "I need you to stay here and keep George calm. And watch the bunnies. These animals are your responsibility. Do you understand?"

The twins nodded in unison.

"Thank you. I'll be right back." *I hope,* she silently added.

She got out and closed the door. The first gust soaked her jeans from the knees down. One of her waterproof boots had a crack in its sole, so her right sock became instantly soggy. And cold.

Lynette had hosted a baby shower here many years earlier that Kara had attended. So she was vaguely familiar with the lay of the land.

Shivering, she ran to the front door. Locked, of course. No potted plants or doormat to look under—the most logical places to hide a key, she figured. Next, she tried the garage door. Again, no luck. She hurried around the gravel path to the kennel. She knew some home owners hid a spare key in the doghouse because they figured most burglars would be afraid to enter the pen.

George's doghouse was big enough for her to crawl into. She got on her knees and shined the light inside. No key. She even checked under the thick pad. There was rainwater pooled near the threshold but the cushion seemed completely dry. Brad had been right about that. George would stay cozy and snug in his bed, but the wind echoed frighteningly under the roof. The sound gave her goose bumps.

Stubbornly, she pressed on, making her way around several overturned pieces of patio furniture to the elegant French doors that she remembered led to the living room. The doors jiggled slightly, but didn't open.

She was just about ready to give up when she saw it—a window that was slightly ajar. She wiped the rain from her face and hurried closer. It wasn't a big window. And she still hadn't lost that extra ten pounds of baby weight. Could she fit through?

What other choice did she have? She couldn't imagine sending Sophie or Sadie into a strange home alone, nor could she picture lifting George's one hundred and eighty pounds up to the chest-high sill.

Swearing softly, she stuck her flashlight in her pocket and pushed upward with all her might. Unlike the warped wooden, single-pane pieces of crap at her rental house, this vinyl-clad window opened with ease. She rose up on her tiptoes to look inside.

The laundry room.

She pulled herself up onto the sill with less effort than she'd expected—carrying her twins must have given her more upper body strength than she'd guessed. Unfortunately, she couldn't quite reach the dryer to use as leverage. She was folded across the opening like a melted sandwich.

Wiggling as carefully as possible to avoid shredding her cheap plastic raincoat, she maneuvered sideways—sweating and puffing like a woman who'd just given birth. With supreme effort and contortionist ability she didn't know she possessed, she finally managed to get one leg in before losing her balance. A large pile of dirty clothes broke her fall.

Breathing hard, she inhaled the scent of man and boy. Smells she couldn't place in her life, but could instinctively identify. Sweat, kitchen odors, wet dog.

Oh, wait, that last is probably from me.

She got up, closed the window and turned on the light. "At least there's power," she muttered. "If the police come, they'll be able to see who they're arresting."

She used a towel from the pile to wipe her boots, then hurried into the kitchen, pausing a moment to get her bearings. "Too neat," she murmured, glancing about the room. "Don't they ever eat here?"

Shaking her head, she dashed to the front of the house, switching on every light she passed. The wide entry was as she remembered it, and to her great relief, the lock was a simple dead bolt, not some intricate alarm unit. She pulled up her hood and opened the door, intending to run to her car for George. Instead, she let out a scream and jumped back.

A man was standing in front of her. A man with dripping wet hair, a key in one hand and a lantern dangling from the other.

The lights stayed on just long enough for her mind to process that the man was Brad. Then, suddenly, they were enveloped in blackness.

"Damn," Brad swore, feeling for the switch on the battery-operated lantern he'd been carrying for the past couple of hours. The restaurant and surrounding neighborhood had been without power since shortly after he'd spoken with Kara.

The weak yellowish glow was powerful enough to brighten the entry. He looked at the woman in front of him. He hadn't meant to frighten her. When he'd driven up and seen her car—plus spotted lights on inside the house—he'd figured that she'd managed to get in. He had no idea how, but if he hadn't managed to close the latch on George's kennel properly, then maybe he'd left a door ajar, too.

"I was hoping to get unloaded before we lost power. How'd you get in? Did I forget to lock up?"

Kara dropped her chin and shook her head. "Open window in the utility room."

"You broke in? Why?"

"I...George... The road to the coast is always the first to go, you know. I'm sorry. I shouldn't have."

"Dad? Can I come in now?" a voice shouted over the wind.

"Wait a second. Let me get some candles going."

"Is that your son? I have a flashlight. He can bring George in with him."

She slipped past him before he could stop her. His mind was still trying to process arriving home after boarding up Willowby's to find her here. He turned on the heel of his rubber boot to follow.

Justin appeared out of the wet gloom. "Is that the lady from the dog wash place?"

"It's called The Paws Spa," a little girl's voice said succinctly.

A moment later, a tiny sprite in a pink Barbie raincoat stepped into the light. "Our mommy owns it," she said, her voice proud and slightly challenging.

"Woof."

George's greeting made Brad smile, despite the

fact he was ready to drop from fatigue. "Hello, George. I take it you convinced Kara you were too afraid to stay in your kennel alone, huh?"

"Come on, Dad," Justin said. "Mom always brought him into the laundry room when there was a storm. She probably didn't tell you because you would have made him go back outside, but he gets scared. Especially when the power goes out."

Brad scowled. Thanks, Lynette. You could have told me, instead of making me look like a heartless fiend.

He eyed the two little girls and their mother, who were all watching him intently. "Fine. He can come inside. Where we all should be. Only crazy people stand around in the rain on a night like this."

"Oh," Kara said in surprise. "Thanks for the offer, but we have to go. Wilma's expecting us."

Kara passed him George's loaner leash. Her hand was wet and ice-cold. Impulsively, he put both of his around hers and squeezed gently. "You're soaking. At least, dry off first. You'll come down with pneumonia." When she hesitated, he added, "And if you're talking about the Donning farm, you should call and make sure the road's still open. We used to buy produce from them, and I've seen the Gage Road grade turn into a skating rink when the temperature drops."

She shook off his hold. "I'd planned on taking the long way around. Besides, it's not just us. We have a whole menagerie."

"The bunnies," one little girl said.

"And Frida Kahlo, our turtle," the other added.

"You have a turtle named after a Mexican artist?"

Kara smiled. "You should see the colorful markings on her belly. She's very special."

Softly, he asked, "How do you know it's a female?"

"I don't. Luckily, we only have the one, so it shouldn't be an issue."

He laughed, and then motioned for her to follow. "Come in and dry off. Our fireplace runs on propane. It'll be nice and warm in here in a few minutes. Hopefully the phone lines are still up. You can call Wilma and tell her what's happening."

"Mommy, I need to go potty."

"Me, too. I don't think I can hold it."

Kara didn't hesitate for long. "Okay. I really do need different socks. Let me grab our bag."

"And the bunnies, Mommy," said one as she sat on the floor to remove her boots.

Brad bent down and handed the lantern to the other child. "Wait here. I'll get your rabbits."

Ten minutes later, the Williams family—including pets—was safely inside and drying off by his fireplace with its lovely fake fire. George had made himself at home on the large area rug in front of the sofa. Even Justin had stuck around instead of disappearing down the hall to his room or the addition. Brad looked around and smiled. For the first time in what seemed like forever, his house felt alive.

CHAPTER FIVE

"YOUR DOG SNORES."

"He does, doesn't he?"

Kara sighed. "I can't tell you how embarrassed I am. I broke into your house."

"Yes, you did, didn't you?" he said, smiling.

Kara had followed Brad into the kitchen after getting the girls settled at the coffee table with their coloring books. The light from the lantern wasn't great but it beat being strapped in a little car in the middle of a big storm.

"Kara, it's no big deal. I left the window open. It's not like you were making off with the plasma TV. But you could have hurt yourself, so if you ever need in for any reason again, my neighbor has a key."

Kara sat down on the same stool she'd used a few minutes earlier when she'd called Wilma.

"Stay in town," her friend had advised. "We have a flood watch all over the place. My driveway looks like a lake. Maybe you should go to your mother's."

Brad was standing at the large gas stove, his back

to her. "I could take the girls to my mother's. She lives in the trailer park near the hospital. It's pretty high. I've never known it to flood."

He turned. "But to get there, you have to go through town. If it's flooding at Wilma's place, there will be bad spots in Pine Harbor, too. And with this wind, there could be power lines down… Stay. Please. It's the least Justin and I can do to repay you for taking such good care of George."

He went back to what he was doing—heating up a pot of soup he'd brought with him from the restaurant. She certainly hadn't expected to dine on Willowby's tonight.

"Your mom's not going to worry about you, is she?" he asked, going to the refrigerator, which was at least twice as big as hers.

"No. She thinks we're at Wilma's and wouldn't be expecting a call. In fact, she might have had to go to work. I can imagine what a mess the phone lines will be."

"That's right. She works for the phone company, doesn't she? I talk to her once a year about my Yellow Pages ad. She always identifies herself as Kara Jayne Williams's mother."

Kara snickered softly. "That's funny. I wonder if she thinks the connection will mean an easier sell."

"Must work. I buy the same size ad every year—and believe me, it isn't cheap."

"Oh, I know. I was shocked when I first started budgeting advertising costs for The Paws Spa, but with our kind of businesses, people have to be able to reach you on a whim, right?"

"Absolutely."

Neither spoke for a moment, then Brad said, "You know, I'm not surprised by how successful The Paws Spa has become. When you first came to work at the restaurant, I knew you'd do well at whatever you set out to accomplish."

"You did? Really? How?"

"Well, we get a lot of transient help in the food service industry. Kids who want part-time jobs or drifters who hang out for a few months then move on. I could tell from the start that you took it seriously—waitressing wasn't just a way to earn a couple of bucks for a prom dress. You listened, followed orders and never made the same mistake twice."

Kara was touched. And pleased. "Well, thank you. That's nice to know. But you have to admit the mistakes I did make were whoppers. Remember when I filled the saltshakers with sugar?"

"That was you?"

The heat that filled her cheeks made her grateful for the dim light. "Your wife nearly fired me over it, until Reggie told her it was his fault. Apparently, he'd punched a hole in a five-pound bag of sugar and had poured what he could save into baggies—the kind the waitresses used to fill the saltshakers."

He didn't say anything, and Kara got the feeling she'd opened the door to unpleasant memories. Grasping for something to fill the awkward void, she said, "But when you said that, the first thing that came to mind was Fly—the twins' father. Now, there was one awesome mistake."

He looked at her curiously and Kara immediately regretted the bizarre—and very personal—admission. Since he'd moved away from the stove and she felt the sudden need to fidget, she got up, picked up a big, professional-looking ladle and stirred the pot. The aroma of beef, vegetables and herbs filled her senses. "What is this? It smells wonderful."

"Minestrone. Willowby's usual Wednesday night soup. My assistant had it going before the weather announcement." He took a smaller spoon from the drawer and offered her a taste. "Tell me if it needs more pepper."

The scent alone was a powerful lure, but the look in his eyes incited another level of hunger. She opened her mouth and leaned in. "Ummm…delicious. Wow. Is that fresh basil?"

"Always. Well…whenever my delivery guy remembers. I really miss the Donnings' truck farm. Wilma and her husband could always be counted on for the best produce. And mostly organic. They were ahead of their time."

"That's really nice of you to say. I'll tell Wilma when I see her. Hopefully tomorrow. If the roads are open," she added, cocking her head to listen to a wind gust rattle the windows. "It sounds pretty bad, doesn't it?" A shiver passed through her body. This was the kind of weather she dreaded most.

"Are you cold? Why don't you go back in the living room with the kids? I'll bring in a tray for everyone."

"No. I need to keep busy. If I stay distracted, I'm less likely to fall apart, which, believe me, is not a pretty sight."

"I doubt that's true."

She remembered the night she threw herself at Fly. "Hold me," she'd pleaded, burying her face against his chest. "Make me forget."

Shaking her head to dislodge the image, she looked around, squinting against the dim light. "Where do you keep the bowls?"

"Second shelf to the right of the sink."

She moved the candle he'd given her earlier on the marble counter and opened the handsome teak cupboard door he'd pointed to. Just as neat as she'd expected. His kitchen reminded her of Willowby's. "Do you and Justin eat here much?"

"Not really. Usually we eat at the restaurant. I try to fix breakfast for him on my days off, but mostly he prefers cold cereal or a breakfast bar. For the past week, he's had to walk to school, which means even less time in the morning."

She carried five soup bowls to the tray he was preparing. "I heard about the bus incident," she said quietly. "Wilma knows one of the drivers."

"Yeah, well…he's had a few behavior problems since his mother left. And the holidays didn't help."

She wanted to say something, but what did she know about dealing with a teen? She could barely keep up with her five-year-olds. "It's not any of my business and you can take this with a grain of salt—" She grinned, recalling their earlier discussion of her mistake. "But the other day when you said something about finding a new home for George…I don't think—"

"You're going to give away my dog?" a youthful voice shouted from the doorway.

Brad let out a soft groan and faced his son. "Justin, Kara and I were having a private conversation."

"About me. And George."

Kara set down the bowls and walked toward Justin, who was visibly quivering with outrage. "Your dad said that in passing the day George dug his way out of the pen. I'm sure he didn't mean it. I shouldn't have said anything. I'm sorry."

Brad appreciated Kara's attempt to smooth Justin's ruffled feathers, but he could tell his son wasn't listening. Brad could do very little right these days, and no matter what he said, it would be taken the wrong way.

"Kara's right. I'm not getting rid of your dog."

"You better not. If George goes, so do I," Justin snarled, turning on one heel. He marched away, stalking past the twins without acknowledging them.

Brad looked at the little girls, who were holding each other as if waiting for something bad to happen. George was awake again and standing just a few feet behind them, his eyes wide with apprehension, as well. "Wow, that wasn't exactly the best way to spark anyone's appetite, was it?"

Kara went to her daughters. "Let's wash up for supper." She led them to the guest bathroom—a place that had seen more activity tonight than it had in months. He absently wondered if there was even a towel beside the sink.

George followed them with his gaze. When the door closed behind them, he ambled over to Brad and sat down. His cropped ears pointed sharply upward in what Brad called the dog's "Batman motif." When Lynette first brought her newly purchased puppy home, George had been wearing a funny-looking plastic prosthesis designed to keep his ears aligned. She'd been upset because she hadn't wanted their dog to undergo surgery. Unfortunately, the breeder hadn't gotten her message.

"We're never going to show him," she'd complained. "Why put him through the misery?"

Brad had wanted to ask, "If you're never going to show him then why buy a pedigreed dog?" But he'd kept his comment to himself. Brad had actually liked George's upright ears. He thought they added a certain dignity to the otherwise ungainly pup.

"I wasn't serious, George," he said. The dog seemed to read the lie. His right ear, the one with more white than black, tilted downward. A wave of guilt made him feel like a heartless schmuck.

He walked to the dog and went down on one knee. "None of this is your fault, boy. I need to remember that. I'm sorry."

He gave the animal a hug, feeling a little foolish,

but relieved, too. George made a funny gurgling sound and nuzzled the side of Brad's face. Dog saliva, wet and slimy, coated his cheek. He jerked back and reached up to wipe it off, but caught sight of Kara standing at the edge of the circle of light cast from the lantern.

He was embarrassed—until he saw her face. Sweet. Tearful. Approving. She had the kind of look you might see from a person who liked you a lot, who thought you were special despite your faults.

His eyes burned like they did when he roasted jalapeño peppers. His throat constricted. He coughed and jumped to his feet. "Soup's hot. Let's eat." Angling toward the hallway, he hollered, "Justin. Come and get it."

THREE HOURS LATER, Kara finally sank back into the plush comfort of the sofa and let out the sigh that had been building ever since she opened the door and found Brad there. What a crazy night! Not at all the way she'd planned her escape from the storm, but, fortunately, the distractions— playing Jenga and Dora the Explorer dominoes with the twins—had worked. She'd barely even noticed the howling wind and driving rain. Brad's house was well built, and the vaulted ceiling provided an added cushion between Kara and the noise.

"I wonder if we'll get the power back on before morning," her host said. He was relaxing in an over-sized leather armchair, his stocking feet kicked out on the matching ottoman.

Kara glanced at her watch. "I can't believe it's only nine. The twins are usually in bed at eight, but I'm always up till midnight. Now, I can barely keep my eyes open."

She looked at her girls, who were curled up in their secondhand pink and purple Barbie sleeping bags a few feet from the hearth. Justin had just retired to his room—grateful, Kara was certain, to escape his adoring fan club. Sophie and Sadie had decided over the course of the evening that boys weren't so icky after all.

"We like him, Mommy," Sophie had whispered when the three of them had carried their bowls to the kitchen.

"He's pretty," Sadie added.

Pretty intense, Kara had been tempted to say, but she'd held her comment. The teen had a lot to deal with. And there definitely seemed to be a gulf of strong feelings between Justin and his father. At least, on Justin's part.

"Are you sure you don't want me to make up the guest room? I haven't checked on the conditions back there in a while, but it would give you more privacy."

Kara smiled drowsily. "This is perfect. The fire. A snoring dog that sounds like a wild beast in the forest—just how I always imagined camping would be."

He snickered. "Can I get you a sleeping bag at least? The twins look pretty cozy in theirs."

Through droopy eyes, she took in the scene before her. Her daughters asleep on the floor a safe distance from the fire, their turtle's glass-walled home sitting on one side of the raised hearth, the bunny hutch with a stack of newspapers under it on the other. "We've really made ourselves at home, haven't we?"

Before he could reply, she added, "I'm fine. Thank you. This couch is the softest thing I've ever sat on." She pulled the thick woolen throw up to her chin and nestled into a cocoon of warmth.

"Sometimes Sadie gets restless and wakes up in the night. If she does, I'll just move down there beside her. Don't worry. I'm plenty comfortable."

"Good. Then, I'll head off to bed, too. I'm sure tomorrow is going to be a big mess." He stood up, pausing beside George, who was sleeping peacefully not far from the girls. "I should probably take him out one more time, and then make a bed for him in the laundry room."

Kara sat up. "Couldn't he stay here?" she asked. "He makes me feel safe."

Brad looked at her. "Safe from what?"

She dropped her chin. "I...I don't handle storms well."

"What do you mean? You seem okay to me."

"I am okay as long as I'm busy or preoccupied. And I try to be brave for the girls, but when it's just me and the night, and the wind, and the lightning..." She shook her head. "Not so much. But I feel better having George around." She leapt to her feet and walked to where Brad was standing. "I'll take him out to pee then dry him off really well before I bring him back inside, okay?"

"Sure. I guess." He touched her arm, stopping her. "Have you always been afraid of storms?"

She nodded. "My dad died on a night like this."

"I'm sorry. I shouldn't have asked. It's none of my business, but you seem so strong and capable, I can't imagine anything scaring you."

Lightning momentarily lit the room. "Ah, well, that just proves how wrong appearances can be. I mean, George might be scared, too, but to me he's a living, breathing security blanket."

He looked at her oddly, and it suddenly struck her that she was asking a lot of the man—a virtual stranger. Her children and pets were camped out in his living room and now she was asking to break some kind of house rule where his dog was concerned.

"Oh, dang, I really am pushy, aren't I? Talk about taking advantage… I'm sorry. He's your dog and if you want him in the laundry—"

He stopped her. "Habit. I never knew Lynette allowed George inside during storms. I grew up in a household where an animal's place was outdoors." He grimaced. "I set up the same rules when we got George. Apparently, Lynette didn't agree."

"Why didn't she just tell you? Why go behind your back?"

He shrugged. "I have no idea—sort of the story of my marriage, I guess."

His bitterness was impossible to miss.

"So…um…you're okay with him being here?"

He looked at George, who was still sound asleep, barrel chest lifting and falling in the glow from the fireplace. "He's pretty well-mannered, isn't he? Doesn't beg for food. Never gave the rabbits or the turtle a second sniff. I guess all those obedience classes paid off."

He stared at the dog a minute longer then turned to Kara and said, "You know, when I suggested finding him a new home, I wasn't just thinking of myself. He might be happier with another family. One that has time to spend with him."

Kara heard the defeat in his voice. Her instinct was to comfort him, but in her peripheral vision she saw her daughters snuggled close together, reminding her she could only take care of her own. She wasn't going to turn into her mother, taking on every lost cause that came her way.

"George is a very special animal. Smart and intuitive. He can sense how unhappy you and Justin are, but he loves you. You're his people. I'm not an animal psychic, but my guess is he'd pick you over a new family."

He looked into her eyes. "Then why does he run to you every chance he gets?"

"My organic doggie snacks?" she teased.

"I doubt it. I think he knows you have a kind

heart and would never turn him away. He's smart and intuitive, remember?" His grin told her he enjoyed using her words to prove his point, but he didn't give her a chance to reply. "Sleep well, Kara," he said before disappearing into the darkness. "You're safe here. I promise."

She walked to the window and pressed her forehead against the cold glass. She couldn't see the storm, but she felt the driving wind pummel the house. *Safe,* Kara knew, was a relative term. She'd been safe the night her father had died, but her life had changed irrevocably.

She turned and tiptoed past George. He'd let her know if he needed to go outside. She picked up the blanket and a couple of cushions from the sofa and then curled up beside her daughters on the floor. She was in a strange house with her hunky, unhappy ex-boss and his angsty teenage son while a wild storm raged outside.

Sleep? Not likely.

CHAPTER SIX

THE SOUND OF A DOG barking woke her.

George's deep, room-quaking "Woof" made her bolt upright, remembering too late that she'd been sleeping on the floor, not her soft bed. Every muscle in her body cried out in protest.

"George?" she croaked groggily, blinking against the bright sunlight pouring in through the wide-open drapes. Good grief. She'd not only fallen asleep, she'd slept well past daybreak.

She looked around, trying to get her mind in gear. The girls' sleeping bags were empty. And so, she realized in abject horror, was the bunny hutch.

"Sadie. Sophie," she called out, stumbling to her feet. "Where are you?"

"In here, Mommy," Sophie hollered. "No, George, no. Don't eat him."

This was followed by a panic-filled scream that made Kara race toward the sound. The formal dining room. A dusty cherrywood table. Six chairs. Two children on hands and knees crawling furiously to catch up to the huge dog doing a combat crawl toward a silver-brown lop-eared rabbit thumping nervously under the center of the table.

"No, George," Kara cried. "Bad dog."

George froze, his muzzle just inches from Floppy, the eldest of the rabbit clan.

Sadie, her pink nightgown bunched around her knees, darted in and scooped Floppy into her skinny little arms. But backing out was no easy task given the rotund girth of the animal she carried.

Sophie emerged first. She snapped her hands on her hips and glared at Kara. "Mommy, you shouldn't yell at George. Sadie let the bunnies out on accident and George was helping us find them."

Sadie stood up, rocking slightly to get her balance. Floppy dangled to her knees, his powerful hind legs pedaling air. Kara dashed to her and took the rabbit, giving Floppy some support so he didn't accidentally scratch her.

"I thought George was going to bite Floppy," the other twin explained, "but he just used his mouth to move him. We didn't want Floppy to hide under that thing with the other bunnies." She pointed at an elegant corner hutch filled with china.

Kara's stomach rose and fell, picturing the disaster that might have occurred if George and the girls had tried to extricate the rabbits from beneath it. Sweat broke out under her armpits.

"Leave them for now. Girls, back into the living room. George, come."

She bit down on her lip to keep from smiling as

she watched the big dog back up. The chair he was under wobbled several times but didn't fall over. Finally, he was free. He stood up and gave a little shake. She could almost hear him saying, "Whoa, that was hairy."

Impulsively, she went to his side and leaned down to whisper in his ear. "I should have known you were too much of a gentleman to eat a bunny. Sorry, my friend."

"Is everything okay?"

She spun around. Not Brad. Justin. He rubbed his eyes with the heels of his hands.

"Fine. Just a little rabbit crisis. Is your dad still asleep?"

He shook his head. "He woke me up to tell me that school was cancelled and he was going to the restaurant to check on the damage. I think his cell phone is working again. You can call him if you want."

She would. Soon. First…she held Floppy out toward Justin. "Would you mind helping out a minute? Put this guy away while I get his escaped family members."

She didn't really give him an option. She shoved the animal into his arms then dropped to her knees and put her cheek on the floor in front of the cabinet. Even in the dim light, she could see Franny and Moppet huddled together. The twins joined her. But Kara sensed another presence, as well. Just overhead. Warm, moist breath of a dog.

"Back up, George. We've got this under control."

It was another fifteen minutes before she actually felt like she could say that and mean it—once the bunnies were all boxed up and in her car. The sky was clear but the wind had a decided nip to it. The terrarium, which was sitting by the door, would be the last thing to go in the trunk. Both Barbie sleeping bags were neatly rolled up. Every single sock, barrette and wisp of pink had been shoved into one of their three backpacks. And nearly every game piece had been accounted for.

The Williams family was ready to leave. But Kara hated to go without first talking to Brad. Plus, she didn't feel right about leaving Justin alone. But so far Brad hadn't answered his cell phone.

"Why don't I make breakfast while we're waiting for your dad to call me back? Pancakes, anyone?"

The twins shrieked in delight. Pancakes and French toast were their favorite weekend food. Kara could whip up a batch in no time, given the right ingredients.

To her surprise, Justin, who hadn't said much during their chaotic packing episode, actually nodded with enthusiasm. "We have syrup. Dad used to make waffles on his days off. And crepes on special occasions. I like mine with applesauce and syrup."

The combination sounded awful to her but she tried not to show it. "Crepes are a little outside my realm of experience, but I'm told I make a mean pancake."

"They're not really mean," Sophie said, climbing on a stool at the island counter. "She's kidding."

"Uh-huh," Sadie added, obviously undecided about whether to sit near Justin or move the stool. "Sometimes she uses chocolate chips to make smiley faces."

Kara wondered if that sounded equally repulsive to Justin, but he jumped to his feet. "We have chocolate chips."

After just a little hunting, he was able to produce a bag that looked as though it had been untouched at least since his mother lived there. "Cool," Kara said. "Shake out a bunch and you can make the faces."

"I want to."

"Me, too."

Kara sighed. "Sorry, girls. This griddle is built-in. And you know the rule. No helping near the stove when it's on. Justin is older and has longer arms so he can do this safely."

The twins didn't seem pleased to relinquish a job Kara usually let them do when they were home. Her tiny kitchen had an apartment-size stove and only two of the burners worked. Usually, she'd let them design their own pancakes then she'd cook them.

She was just ready to flip the first batch when Brad showed up—with two large coffees, three cartons of chocolate milk and a pink bakery box. "Oh, darn, I'm too late. You're cooking."

"Yep. Pancakes. But coffee is always welcome. There's every high-tech cooking gadget imaginable in this kitchen, but I couldn't find a coffeepot."

"Lynette was a tea drinker and I'm too lazy to make a pot for myself, so I usually buy my fix at the

Pine Harbor bakery, which, as you can see, is up and running," he said. He passed out the milks and greeted the kids, then took a mug from the cupboard and emptied one of the containers into it. "I gambled and bought you a mocha. Hope that works."

She flipped the pancakes then took a sip. "Perfect. Thanks."

Justin made a scoffing sound. She saw Brad flinch but he didn't say anything. He pulled off the plastic lid of the second cup and sampled his. "Not as good as Willowby's, but not bad."

"Speaking of the restaurant," Kara said, after another taste. "Is everything okay? No damage?"

He sat down on a stool beside Sadie, who had made Sophie move over to sit next to Justin. She inched a bit closer to her sister. Being friendly around an intimate fire apparently was one thing, sitting beside a big man in the light of day another. "Not bad. Some water leaked in around two of the doors, but the damage was minimal. John—my second in command—is airing things out. I told him we'd be out later," he said to Justin. "We'll be open tonight."

"When Justin told me school had been cancelled, I phoned Wilma. She said a couple of roads got washed out and the school buses couldn't get through. Apparently the inland areas got hurt worse than the coast."

Brad grabbed the plates Justin had set out and held each for her as she dished up the six smiling pancakes. Once she was done helping the girls put butter and syrup on theirs, he told her, "The town got hit pretty hard, too. The elementary school has a bunch of broken windows. And the bowling alley lost part of its roof."

She returned to the stove and made five circles with the rest of her batter. Even with her back to him, she could sense there was something he wasn't telling her. Something bad.

"You…um…didn't have a chance to drive by The Paws Spa, did you?"

"Yeah, I did. I figured you would be worried. There was some debris across the road at Burney and Western Avenue, but a crew was working on it. Your building looks fine. I got out and walked around, but I didn't break in," he said dryly. "So I'm not sure how the interior fared."

Her cheeks heated at the allusion to finding her inside his home last night, but when she turned to look at him, he winked to let her know he was joking.

His grin left her feeling flustered and distracted. She quickly spun back to check on her pancakes. There was something very intimate about sharing breakfast with a man—even with three children present. Her hand shook slightly as she slid the spatula under one crispy edge and peeked at the bottom. "We might not have many clients if people can't get around, but at least we won't have to spend the day cleaning up mud. Been there, done that, haven't we, girls?"

"The door blew in," Sophie mumbled, through her partially masticated mouthful.

"It was very messy," Sadie added after swallowing then neatly wiping her lips.

Kara piled the last batch on a serving plate and turned off the stove. "Last December. Remember that big storm that hit a week or so before Christmas? Our front door blew in. Ripped off all the trim. Mud came over the threshold. It was bad. But Santa brought Mommy a new door, didn't he?"

Sophie shook her head. "Gramma Nan's boyfriend did, not Santa."

"His name is Tony," Sadie clarified.

Brad chuckled and helped himself to a stack of pancakes. "I know him. He's done some odd jobs at the restaurant." To Kara, he said, "These smell great."

She frowned. There was still something he wasn't telling her. She sipped her coffee and managed a couple of bites while everyone else finished eating. Once the girls and Justin had been excused to take George outside, she looked at Brad and said, "Okay, tell me the rest."

He let out a sigh. "These were great. If I did breakfast at Willowby's, I'd hire you...." He let the suggestion drop. "I drove past your house. You're still renting that place just off Hunter Street, right? The little blue house?"

"How'd you know?"

"Lynette had me drop off an invitation to a baby shower way back when. And a few weeks ago I took the shortcut to the junior high and saw your car parked in the driveway. Your logo is hard to miss."

It wasn't all that surprising that he knew where she lived. Pine Harbor was still small enough to impart a close feeling of community, although the new developments in outlying areas were changing that.

"The roof took a pounding. At a glance, I'd say maybe half the shingles were gone. Maybe it isn't so bad around back, but from the street it looked ugly."

Kara let out a soft groan. She'd just let her renter's insurance lapse. She'd figured what little she and the girls owned could be replaced for less than she was paying in premiums. That might have been a mistake.

"Thank goodness we weren't there last night. That would have been pretty scary, huh?"

His brows knitted in a way that told her he could picture their terror all too easily. His empathy made her uncomfortable. She wasn't used to other people—men—worrying about her.

She shrugged and finished wiping down the marble counter. "Well, on the bright side, maybe this will finally make my landlord replace the roof. It springs new leaks every time it rains. The girls started naming the water spots on their ceiling when the most recent one showed up. I swear it looks just like Stitch—the Disney character from the movie…" She stopped her babbling when she noticed his frown. "What else? Is there more?"

He cocked his head. "No. I'm just confused. Are you really this laid-back when bad things happen or are you hiding your true feelings beneath a facade of calm?"

He didn't know exactly what he'd expected her to do when he broke the news, but this eerie acceptance wasn't the response he'd imagined. When he'd first seen the damage to Kara's house, he'd felt ill. All sorts of terrible images had flashed before his eyes. The girls crushed beneath sodden timbers and shingles. Kara terrified and alone. Dead bunnies and a flattened turtle. His stomach had nearly rejected his first coffee of the day.

"Of course, I'm not happy to hear that my meager possessions are probably ruined, but I won't know the extent of the damage until I see it for myself." She didn't look at him. "But, thanks to you, at least my children and their pets are safe."

She plunged the plastic mixing bowl into the soapy water in the sink and started scrubbing. "And, no matter how bad it is, we'll be okay. Like I told you last night, I've lived through worse."

Her father's death. He understood. He'd lost his father, too. But he still felt her attitude seemed too positive and her mood too chipper to be real. "I wish I had your equanimity. I was awake before dawn worrying about how much damage Willowby's had sustained and how that would affect my ability to open up tonight."

"I'd probably be a basket case if it had been The Paws Spa or if I'd been in my house last night," she said while rinsing the bowl under a stream of water, "but at least the people I care about are okay. Wilma's driveway is a soggy mess, but she still has her late husband's four-wheel drive truck. She said she'd meet me at work. And my mom is fine. The trailer park lost a tree, but it missed all the homes, and she made enough money in overtime to get her car out of impound." She held up one dripping hand. "Don't ask. But, just in case you're ever tempted, don't date a person with alcohol issues."

Brad understood. He'd heard that Tony had a bit of a drinking problem. Nice guy. Good at what he did—unless… "Thanks for the warning, but Tony's not my type."

Her wide grin nearly stopped his heart.

"Now, am I looking forward to hassling with my landlord to get my roof fixed? Heck, no. He's the cheapest cheapskate on the planet, but until I actually see the damage, I'm not going to get too worked up about it."

She picked up a towel and started drying the bowl, fast and furiously. Perhaps she wasn't as calm as she pretended. Or maybe it was the mention of her landlord. "Whose building is it? Not Morris Jakes's, I hope." The man was a scumbag who owned half of the older part of town, where Kara's house was located.

"Unfortunately, yes."

One of Brad's favorite waiters had rented from Morris—until his wife got sick with a terrible sinus infection that the doctor blamed on her living conditions. He started to relate the cautionary tale, but stopped when Kara turned to him and said, "No matter what happens, I can deal with it because last night I slept through the storm. All night. You have no idea what a miracle that is. If some of our stuff got damaged or ruined...it's only stuff. The girls and I are safe—thanks to you."

He barely knew this woman and her children, yet recalling the image of her dilapidated house with the roof half-caved-in made him uneasy. He didn't want her to have to face that alone. "There are a lot of trees down between here and your part of town. Do you want me to drive you home?"

"No, thanks. You've done enough. I'm still a little shocked that you didn't have me arrested for breaking and entering," she said, her smile telling him she was teasing. "I appreciate everything, Brad, but we'd better get home and start cleaning up. Knowing Morris, he'll throw a little plastic tarp over it and call it done."

Brad didn't like the sound of that. If he owned that property, he'd bulldoze the hovel and build something safe. Kara deserved better. A lot better.

After Kara and the girls left a few minutes later, he and Justin put on their boots and walked the perimeter of the house to make sure the property hadn't sustained any damage. Some limbs were down. The patio furniture had gotten tossed about. And the carpet in the guest room in the addition was soaked. The glass wasn't broken, though, which told Brad a window had been left open.

He hadn't been in the addition in weeks. He knew Justin liked to hang out there after school. The pool table and big-screen TV in the main room had been popular draws when Lynette had been here.

Despite Brad's rule—no friends in the house unless Brad was present—he suspected that other kids often accompanied Justin home after school. Was that why the window was open? Did Justin let his friends sneak into the house?

He didn't want to think so, but considering how poorly he and his son communicated, anything was possible.

He went to the garage for his toolbox. When he returned to the addition, he said, "I'm thinking about installing an alarm system."

Justin, who was sprawled in a beanbag chair playing a video game, looked up. "What?"

"Kara got in here pretty easy. Our neighbors aren't that close and we're gone a lot. An alarm might be a good idea."

"We've got George."

Brad glanced around. He wondered where the dog was. Outside in his pen, he hoped. "George wouldn't be much help if someone climbed through this window," he said, using a flat bar to pry the carpet away from the tack strip against the wall. "He can't even see this part of the house. He'd probably never bark."

A suspicious blush crept up Justin's cheeks. He hunched his shoulders as if attempting to disappear. That was all Brad needed to be sure that his guess was right. Justin had been letting his friends in through this window. The thought concerned him.

Were they playing pool and messing around or could there be more? Drugs? Brad was glad he and Lynette had never kept hard alcohol in the house. He'd bring a bottle of wine home on special occasions but that was the extent of their drinking.

His first impulse was to confront his son, but without proof, all he'd get was a denial and a fight. Something had to change, but short of cloning himself, he had no idea how to be in two places at once.

"Have you talked to your mom lately?"

Justin didn't glance up. "Yeah."

"Did you ask her about visiting over spring break?"

The length of the pause told Brad the subject wasn't his best choice. Which Brad had more or less surmised since Lynette hadn't called him personally to work out the arrangements.

"She said now wasn't a good time. Reggie has a new job and they only have one car so she couldn't take me around during the day and stuff. She said I'd be bored out of my mind."

In paradise? "I'm sorry. You were looking forward—"

Justin made a rude sound. "Doesn't matter. Grandma and Grandpa are coming to Uncle Bob's in Portland over the President's Day weekend. She said they'd send me a train ticket and I could hang with the cousins."

And when exactly was she going to clear this with me? He didn't ask the question out loud. The one thing he felt he and Lynette had done right in this divorce was avoid a custody battle over Justin. They'd both agreed that their son needed the stability and continuity Brad could provide. Reggie had wanted to start over in another country, and Lynette apparently couldn't wait to go with him. She'd tried to stay connected by phone and a few sporadic e-mails, but Brad was afraid part of Justin's problem stemmed from a feeling of abandonment. And he honestly couldn't blame him.

KARA DOVE INTO THE CLEANUP at her house like she did everything—with resignation and resolve. It didn't do any good to complain, she'd told her daughters. "This is what happened and this is what we have to do."

Brad had been right—the damage was extensive. A twenty-foot section of her roof was missing—the shingles gone and tar paper peeled back like the skin on a grape. Fortunately, the damage was confined to the front of the house. Unfortunately, the wind had been coming from that direction and rainwater had soaked through the attic, causing the ceiling to collapse in certain places. The twins' bedroom had gotten the worst of it.

The girls had tried to help, but softhearted Sadie would break down in tears every time she ran across one of her stuffed animals—soaked and covered with pasty Sheetrock and insulation, and Sophie fretted about whether or not their clothes could be salvaged.

Finally, in desperation, Kara had called Esmeralda. "Can the girls come over early? If I don't get this cleaned up before my first appointment, I'll be at it all night."

Her neighbor's house, which had a new roof, had escaped unscathed, but because Esmeralda always had a full load of kids in the mornings, Kara hadn't wanted to bother her with two more.

"Of course. Send them over. I'm making meatball soup for lunch. You come, too."

Tears blurred her vision for a second. She was lucky to have such great friends. Wilma had fired up her late husband's four-wheel drive truck to drive into town so she could reschedule their morning appointments at The Paws Spa. Kara had insisted that she could still work this afternoon, but, now, looking at what was left to be done, she wasn't sure.

Her landlord had been by earlier with a couple of guys to cover the roof with a thick blue tarp. When she'd asked for a hand with the interior cleanup, he'd shrugged and walked away. "You're not the only tenant who has damage," he'd snapped. "You need to get your stuff out of here and find another place to stay. That roof might not be safe."

Having learned a few things about building from her uncle, Kara had crawled into the attic before Morris had arrived. Structurally, the rafters were fine. Only the outer layer of tar paper and forty-year-old shingles needed replacing.

"The basic structure is solid. If you'd have gotten

new shingles on it when I asked, my daughters' clothes and bedding wouldn't be soaked. What got wet will wash. We're not going anywhere."

They'd argued for a few minutes before he'd driven off in a huff. Unfortunately, he was right about one thing—the place was barely habitable. For now, she could move the girls into her room, but could she count on her landlord to make the needed repairs quickly? Mildew and mold were valid health concerns in this situation.

The sound of a car pulling into her driveway made her stop stuffing wet clothes into a plastic garbage bag. She walked to the window. She recognized the vehicle immediately. Her mother must have gotten it out of impound that morning.

"Kara?"

"In here, Mom," Kara answered.

A loud gasp was followed by a groan. "Oh, honey, what a mess. Where are the girls?"

"Next door. Are you on your lunch break?"

Nan nodded. "One of the line crew told me your house was damaged. Thank God you weren't here last night. I know how much you hate storms and this…" She made a sweeping motion. "Where were you? You didn't say."

"At…um…a friend's." She hoped her mother would assume she meant Wilma's. "I just tried your cell. It went right to voice mail."

"I unplugged everything when the power went out, including the charger. It's still at home."

Kara wondered if that was the truth or if Tony had run up her bill. Again. She didn't ask. She had enough problems without worrying about her mother's finances.

"Where's Tony? I called the house, too. I thought maybe he'd help. You know Morris. Throw a tarp up and walk away is his idea of fixing the place."

Her mother didn't answer right away, then, with a resigned sigh, she admitted, "He's in a treatment center. His lawyer told him it might make a difference between jail time and probation. Tony swears this is it. He's going to clean up his act."

Kara had her doubts but she knew this wasn't the time to share them with her mother. Nan's eyes had bluish bags under them, and she seemed more fragile and nervous than usual. "What are you going to do?" Nan asked. "Do you and the girls want to move in with me? Obviously you can't stay here."

Kara hated being told she couldn't do something. And, even though Tony was currently locked up in rehab drying out, he would come back, and more than likely he would start drinking again. Kara would never—ever—knowingly put her children in close proximity to a drunk. She'd lived through the horror of that herself with her mother's disastrous second husband.

"Thanks for the offer, Mom, but if I give an inch, Morris will take a mile. He's been trying to get me out of here for months. This is just the kind of opportunity he'd seize, and I'd be screwed." She looked at her daughters' ceiling. At least now the stain that looked like Stitch was gone. "Wilma has a portable heater and a couple of fans for me to borrow. Once we dry the place out, how hard can it be to replace the Sheetrock? Morris will have to repair the roof eventually."

Nan looked around, her expression dubious. "But, honey, you're not a carpenter. Damn that uncle of yours for making you think you can do everything yourself."

"Uncle Kurt was the best person I've ever known. He taught me to believe in myself, Mom. What do you want me to do? Sit around wringing my hands until some guy on a white horse shows up? How often has that happened to you?"

Nan let out a huff of frustration and shook her head. "I'm just saying you try to do too much. At least send the girls over to my place. There's no reason they have to suffer."

Kara closed her eyes. The screen in her mind filled with an image of her stepfather in an alcoholic rage raising his closed fist to her. Tony wasn't Doug, she told herself. And he wasn't currently residing with her mother. But Kara couldn't protect her daughters if she wasn't with them. "They're five, Mom. They think this is an adventure, but I would really, really appreciate it if you'd take the bunny family and Frida Kahlo home with you."

"The turtle?"

"I could keep them at The Paws Spa, but…"

Nan waved away her explanation. "I can use the company with Tony gone. Let's load them up. Are you sure you don't want the girls to come, too? I have to go back to work this afternoon, and I didn't get much sleep last night, but—"

Kara cut her off. "See? This is best. Just babysitting my pets will help a lot." She hugged her mother. "Thanks for offering."

Nan left minutes later—animals, food and written instructions about how to care for them, included. Kara worked furiously until her car was filled with plastic bags of wet bedding, clothes and towels. She hadn't told her mother that the bathroom was virtually unusable, but she was lucky, The Paws Spa had a pristine toilet, shower and washer and dryer. Worst-case scenario, she and the girls would run back and forth between their house and her place of business until things got back to normal.

"Wilma, I'm here," she called, lugging two bags with her as she stumbled through the door of The Paws Spa.

She was greeted by a cacophony of barks. Early arrivals or clients Wilma hadn't been able to re-schedule? She hurriedly shoved a load of size-five clothes into the washer, then donned her smock and raced back to the main area. "Wilma?"

"Over here," the older woman called. "I started without you." A second later, she added gruffly, "Might have been a mistake."

Kara burst out laughing. "Oh, no, not Prin," she cried, half chuckling, half groaning. "Not today."

Prin—or Princess Polly Cartland's Miss, according to her AKC registration—was an eight-year-old, purebred sheepdog who considered herself royalty. Wilma called her a royal pain in the butt. And didn't think much better of the dog's owners.

Wilma, who had a crown of bubbles in her silver hair, muttered breathlessly as she hosed down the large dog, who squirmed under the spray. "I tried to reschedule her, but do you know what Mrs. B-I-T-C-H said?"

Kara rushed to help. "What?"

"'Bad weather is no excuse for bad service. If you can't accommodate us, we'll find someone who can.'"

Kara shook her head. Prin's owners were new to the area and loaded. They were exactly the demographic she was targeting with her high-end services. Too bad they had to be such jerks.

"I should have been here sooner. I'm sorry. My mom dropped by to give me her input on what I should do." She took the spray nozzle from Wilma and adjusted the control. Kara had already learned that Prin responded best to soft and gentle. She praised the animal and slowly got the dog to stand still while she rinsed the rest of the soap from Prin's thick, tangled coat.

"Did she ask you to stay with her?"

"Yep."

"Did you tell her not as long as she had a drunken loser living with her?"

A bit harsh, but Wilma rarely minced words. "Nope."

"How come?"

"Well, for one thing, Tony isn't there right now. He's in rehab. For another, I shouldn't automatically assume that because he drinks, he becomes violent. The fact that my first stepfather was abusive doesn't mean Tony is, but would I leave the girls alone with him? Never. And I think Mom knows that even if we've never talked about the subject openly. This is the first time she's invited them to spend the night since Tony moved in with her. What does that tell you?"

Wilma didn't reply. They'd had this discussion before. "So what are you going to do?"

"Fix up my place. Did you bring the space heaters?"

"Yup. Do you want me to take the rabbits and turtle? Give you a couple less worries."

"And let your cats carve them up for dinner?" Kara cried with mock horror. "I farmed them out with Mom, but thanks for offering."

"I'll have you know Pooka and Dilbert are well-mannered...compared to this beast."

Kara grabbed one of the giant bath sheets she'd sewn from a bolt of terry cloth and started drying Prin. The dog let out a rumble of pleasure, but a second later—with no warning—she snapped at Kara's hand.

"See?" Wilma said smugly. "What did I tell you?"

True, the animal was spoiled rotten and had very

poor discipline, but Kara couldn't hold Prin's lack of training against her. She gingerly continued the drying process, making sure not to get any body part within nipping range. "Prin is a good girl," she said in a soothing voice. "She can't help it she was raised by twits with too much money and no time to spend teaching their pet nice manners. It's not your fault you're neurotic, is it, sweetie?"

Wilma made a scoffing sound and rolled her eyes. "You only see things the way you want them to be," she said, walking away to prepare the grooming stand.

Kara wondered if that was true. Her uncle had called himself a die-hard optimist. He'd convinced her that with hard work and determination she could accomplish anything. What if he was wrong? Her house was missing part of its roof. Her daughters were going to have to start bathing at a dog-grooming facility. Money she'd had earmarked for her expansion would need to go to repairs until her landlord reimbursed her, which might never happen.

So why am I smiling? She wanted to credit her positive mood to a good night's sleep, but she was honest enough to admit that it was at least in part due to Brad. He'd brought her coffee—a *grande* mocha. For a woman who'd never had a boyfriend who put her needs over his own, this thoughtful gesture was too rare a treat not to smile about.

CHAPTER SEVEN

"GEORGE," BRAD CALLED.

Through the trees to his left he heard an echoing call. "Geor…orge."

By the time he and Justin had realized the dog was gone, it was time to go to work. He didn't expect a big crowd tonight and planned to let his assistant close up, but he still needed to go to Willowby's and make sure everything was up and running. And he'd planned to take Justin with him.

"Any sign of him?" he asked when they met up again.

"Like a trail of cookie crumbs?"

Brad grinned. That was the kind of reply he was used to hearing from his smart-ass son. "Wet paw prints maybe?"

Justin had been following the bike lane that the City Fathers had put in a couple of years earlier. Joggers and visitors to the area also used the trail because it afforded a glimpse of ocean. The shoreline of the Pacific was still a good mile or so in the distance, but inland creeks and runoff had created a marshy wetland between the headlands and the surf.

Brad had chosen to walk a less well-delineated, and far more treacherous, path along the bluff. He'd seen George chase birds in this direction when he was younger.

A few feet away from where they were standing he could see a fresh break along the cliff's edge. Wind and rain from the last storm probably had undermined the bank, making it unsafe. A person—or a very large, heavy dog—could have stepped wrong and tumbled to the rocks below.

He approached cautiously, leaned over the brink where earth met air and looked down. Nothing but car-sized boulders entangled in trees and bushes. He let out a sigh of relief and turned around.

"The bank is really unsafe," he said, returning to where Justin was standing. "Stay on the trail, okay? I should call somebody to post warning signs."

"Were you hoping to find George's body down there?"

Brad cleared the distance between them. "Of course not. What a rotten thing to say. I care about George, and like I tried to tell you last night, I'm not planning on getting rid of him. I get frustrated sometimes, okay? I was used to your mother taking care of him, and I'm not very good at this sort of thing."

Justin didn't say anything. Now, Brad thought, would be the time to bring up Justin's feelings about his mother, but before he could work up the courage, his phone rang. Willowby's.

"Boss, we got a problem," John said. "The health inspector wants us to wipe down all the vents and change every filter. He says the fans we used to dry the carpet might have sent spores or something into the vents."

Brad groaned. "Justin and I will be right there." To his son, he said, "I've got a job for you. A paying job."

"What about George?"

Brad glanced left then right. "In the past when he got out of his pen we could always find him here, right? But not lately. I think that means he's headed back to you-know-where."

"Kara's?"

"Where else?"

"What if the dogcatcher picks him up?"

"We'll check there if she doesn't see him. I promise you, Justin, we'll find him. Now, how much am I paying you to wipe down vents?"

"Twenty bucks an hour?"

"In your wildest dreams."

The two continued haggling over the going rate of child labor as they walked to the house, but in the back of his mind, Brad couldn't help hoping George made it safely to The Paws Spa. Partly, he had to be honest, because that meant he'd get to see Kara again.

He wondered if she was dating anybody. He

hadn't asked anyone out since his divorce—hadn't even thought about another woman. Now, it seemed he couldn't get Kara out of his head.

"HE'S BA…ACK."

Kara clicked off her electric clippers and glanced up from the paw she was trimming. "Who? What?"

"George. Mud from head to tail. For a minute I thought it was a different Great Dane."

Kara looked around. Wall-to-wall clients. They'd never had such a busy afternoon. Three were regulars who'd begged to get Mochi, Zenith and Spam in; plus, they had two new drop-ins that Kara couldn't turn away. She was going to need every penny she could scrounge up to get her house back in order.

"Is he out in the yard?"

Wilma nodded. "I gave him water and tied him up. All our big kennels are in use."

"Good. If he walked all the way here, he's probably tired. I doubt he'll get into trouble while we're finishing up. Oh…and would you call Brad and let him know George is okay? I promised Judy I'd have Missy done by the time she got back from the beauty parlor."

She'd have liked to talk to Brad herself, but that was an indulgence she couldn't afford. This morning she'd sensed an attraction between them that held infinite possibilities. And that was a problem. She wasn't an infinite possibilities kind of girl. She was the mother of twins. Her possibilities were limited by the magnitude of her responsibilities. And, at the moment, she couldn't afford to forget that.

The rest of the afternoon rushed by in a blur. She and Wilma bathed seven dogs, two cats and a guinea pig that had got loose in the storm. The last client belonged to Paula Taylor, an old school friend whose son was a year older than the twins.

"Hey," Paula had asked, "what's this I hear about you and Brad Ralston? Did you really spend the night with him during the storm?"

Kara had scoffed. "And here I thought the phones being out might slow down the gossip. I took George home then couldn't get out again. The roads were too bad. The girls and I slept on the floor in front of his fireplace. Would you please make sure that version of the story gets airtime?"

Her friend had laughed. "I figured as much. Women with five-year-olds don't have the time or energy to mess around."

Paula was right, but that didn't mean they didn't dream of sexy men, firelight and all the romance that went with that vision—minus the kids and the snoring dog.

Unfortunately, she knew she'd be adding to the gossip this evening. When Wilma talked with Brad, he'd suggested Kara and the girls bring George to the restaurant, where he and Justin were diligently working to satisfy some kind of health department edict. "Dinner is on me," he'd said, including Wilma in the invitation.

Kara had thought about saying no—for half a second. Willowby's beat fast food every time. The only downside was the current state of her wardrobe. She and the girls might look like vagabonds from the charity closet, but she wasn't going to let that bother her.

What did bother her was Wilma's adamant refusal to join them. "My cats need me. Pooka is on medication. He can't miss a dose. Plus, I saw a pregnant female stray the other day and I'm afraid she might be living in my barn. If I get home too late, the truck might scare her away. I can't have a litter of dead kittens on my conscience."

Was her best friend turning into one of those weird cat ladies she'd read about? Maybe it was time Wilma got a dog.

"Justin?"

Brad hurried from the kitchen toward the offices where he'd seen his son heading moments earlier. He was expecting Kara and her daughters at any time. He'd already reserved the nicest table and he'd planned to ask Justin if he wanted to join them.

"Son?"

The door to Reggie's office stood ajar. Brad felt the muscles in his abdomen tighten. He seldom had reason to go into the room where Lynette, in a moment of cathartic vomit, had admitted making love to his former best friend and partner.

The thought sickened him and he'd cleaned out

what he needed to run the business then closed the door. He planned to turn the room into a storage area.

The light was on, so he looked inside. Justin was sitting behind the desk staring down at something in his hands. A framed photo.

"Hey, pal, are you hungry? Kara's bringing George. You could eat with her and the twins." Brad tried to keep his voice upbeat, even though he knew what picture his son was looking at. Brad, Lynette and Reggie standing in front of their newly opened restaurant. Back when they were young and filled with hopes and dreams.

He'd never have guessed this was how his life would turn out.

"Why didn't you stop them?"

Good question. One he'd asked himself a thousand times. "By the time I found out, it was too late." He'd felt like such a fool when Lynette told him.

How could I not know? How could anyone be oblivious to such blatant cheating? Because he trusted too much? Or because he was a stupid chump? His son obviously seemed to think it was the latter. "Maybe it had been too late for a long time," he said, walking into the room. He took the photo from Justin's hands and glanced at it. "Your mother wanted something else, someone else. I couldn't change that."

Justin pushed away from the desk. His body visibly trembled with anger. Why, Brad wondered. They'd worked well together all day. Why this sudden change? Was it drugs, a part of him thought. He'd read the literature Justin's teachers had sent home after his son's first brush with trouble. Volatility was one of the indicators, right?

Damn it, Lynette, why aren't you here to help your son? You never let him get away with anything. You'd know what to do.

"Before she left, Mom said she always felt as if she came in second place to Willowby's," Justin said, his eyes narrowed in anger. "Reggie worked here, too, and he didn't make her feel that way."

The accusation was clear. Reggie could run a business and love a woman. Brad couldn't.

He wanted to explain that Reggie lived on the edge, constantly taking risks that probably seemed exciting to a woman who was married to a by-the-book kind of guy. Reggie was the people person. He had the charisma to draw customers in. Brad made sure they had good food to eat. How boring was that?

Before he could say anything, Claudia Mosely, his evening hostess, rapped on the frame of the door. "Your guests are here, Brad. I seated them at table number one, but I'm…um…not sure where to put George."

A large black-and-white head looked around the door. A steady thump, thump, thump signaled a happy greeting. Brad suddenly felt as if a portion of the weight from his shoulders had been lifted. He took George's leash from her, and leaned down to pet the dog.

George's coat was smooth and glossy, and he smelled like a breath of fresh air. "Hello, boy, good to have you back. Nice toes."

Justin, curious, moved around the desk. "They're red. Someone painted his toenails red."

"And hot-pink," Claudia put in, pointing to George's back feet.

Brad and Justin turned to each other. "The twins."

Father and son walked their dog to the empty storeroom where they'd been keeping a dog pad and a few chew toys—just in case—then they headed upstairs. As they passed the kitchen, Brad paused to poke his head inside to make sure everything was under control. He was a few steps behind Justin as they approached the round table overlooking the Pacific.

His eyes missed the view entirely. All he could see was Kara in a fuzzy pink sweater that topped a black turtleneck adorned with candy canes. Her hair was mussed from wind and work, he assumed. She looked tired, but the smile she gave him the moment she spotted them sent a bolt of energy straight to his core.

"Justin," the two girls chimed in harmony, slipping off their chairs to greet him excitedly.

Their delighted expressions changed instantly when his son snarled, "You ruined my dog, you little twits."

The twins' eyes widened in shock before they went to their mother and burst into tears.

Brad reacted without thinking. He grabbed his

son's sleeve when the boy turned to leave. "Justin. That was rude and uncalled for. Apologize."

Justin's eyes narrowed with fury. "No. They shouldn't have done it. He's not their dog."

At some level, Brad understood what this was about. Loss. Losing control over yet another aspect of his life. But that didn't mean he could let his son's bad manners stand.

"I'm sorry, Justin," Kara said, looking up from comforting her daughters. "We should have asked first. The girls just wanted to surprise you. They thought you'd think it was funny."

"This isn't your fault, Kara," Brad said. "Or Sophie and Sadie's." He gave Justin's arm a small shake. "You made two little girls cry, son. Tell them you're sorry."

"But he's my—"

"Tell them."

Justin's chin dropped. His shoulders bunched belligerently, but he shifted around enough to shoot a quick look at the twins. Sadie was on her mother's lap. Sophie stood glaring at him—obviously not expecting much of an apology.

"Sorry," he muttered.

Kara cleared her throat. "Apology accepted. Right, girls? Now, is there any way you'd feel up to joining us? We're starved."

Justin looked at his father. Brad didn't need to be a mind reader to know the boy wanted to disappear. "Actually, Justin still has some homework to finish, so he's going to grab something from the kitchen and eat with George. Right, son?"

Justin nodded and pivoted on one heel.

"Um…Justin," Kara called. "The polish on George's nails is the kid-friendly kind. It'll come off if you rub it with a damp cloth and a little soap. You don't need fingernail polish remover."

The boy muttered a low, "Okay," and left.

Brad glanced around, taking in the curious looks of the half-dozen other guests, before returning his attention to Kara. Her fatigue was more evident than ever. Had her day seemed as long as his? Of course, it had. Her house had suffered considerable damage. And when Wilma had called, she'd said they were swamped.

He pulled out the chair that Sadie had been sitting in. "I'm really sorry about this. Just what you didn't need, right?"

Tears pooled in Kara's eyes, and Brad suddenly wished he could take her in his arms and hold her, make things better. Unfortunately, he couldn't do that. Any public display of affection—no matter how benign—would get back to Justin.

So instead he used a pristine white linen napkin to wipe Sophie's tears, and then handed it to Sadie. "For the record, I thought you both did a very good job of painting George's toes. Who did the pink?"

Sadie lifted her hand shyly.

"Nice."

She beamed for a moment then buried her face in her mother's fuzzy pink sweater.

Brad stood up without meeting Kara's eyes. He knew what he had to do. Justin was hurting enough without adding any new dynamics to the situation. Brad wouldn't risk his troubled son taking out his frustration on these two, darling little girls. The only practical course of action—the best for everyone— was for Brad to stay away from Kara and her daughters.

CHAPTER EIGHT

AFTER A WEEK of juggling makeshift repairs on her house, showering at The Paws Spa and pinching pennies so tightly her fingers hurt, the last thing Kara needed was a fight with her landlord. But she'd known she was in trouble the minute she'd returned from taking the girls to school and found Morris's truck parked in her driveway.

She took the check she'd made out that morning from her purse and walked to the driver's side door of his shiny red Silverado. "Hi, Morris, been waiting long? I kinda expected you later at The Paws Spa."

She'd called him earlier to tell him he could pick up the rent. February first. Right on time.

He shifted uneasily in the seat with hands gripping the steering wheel. "I can't take it, Kara."

"What? Why?" Her spirits lightened immediately. Was he going to acknowledge the work she'd been doing every spare minute for the past week by giving her credit on her rent?

She'd not only ripped out the smelly, curled linoleum in the bathroom and pulled up all of the carpet in the girls' bedroom, she'd hauled away a dozen or more garbage bags of disgusting damp insulation and crumbling wallboard.

"'Cause you gotta get out, Kara. Right away. This weekend."

Kara's buoyant mood disintegrated. "What are you talking about? Move out? For how long?" Maybe he intended to get the place fumigated once the carpenters had the roof fixed.

"Forever."

"Pardon?"

"The kinds of repairs I want to make require the house to be empty, Kara."

Kara crossed her arms defensively. "We've had this discussion before, Morris. You can't kick me out. This place is all I can afford right now."

"It isn't healthy for anyone to live in it. The insurance guy who came to look at the damage told me there was black mold under the floor. You want your daughters to get sick?"

The thought made her queasy but she couldn't trust that he was telling the truth. She suspected Morris had another agenda and was just using this tactic to get her out of the house. He'd tried before. "I don't believe you. We're all fine, except for the fact we're crowded into one room. Show me where it is."

He pulled the Rancher's Feed ball cap a little lower on his forehead. "I got a contractor coming Monday. I told him to tear down any suspicious walls and rip up the floors. That gives you the weekend to get your stuff out. If you don't have your things out of here by then, I won't be responsible."

"The weekend? You're giving me not even three days to find a new place to live, pack my belongings and move? That's insane. There are laws against that. I have rights."

"Not when an insurance company condemns a building. It's out of my hands."

"Like I said, I don't believe you."

He shook his head. "You're just as stubborn as your uncle was," he said, reminding her of the time Kurt chained himself to a logging truck to protest the company's impending sale to an out-of-state conglomerate. "I don't care if you believe me or not. The contractor is coming on Monday, and he's going to tear out every stick of lumber that has even a speck of black mold on it. Walls, floors, ceiling, the whole works. And if he tells me it would be cheaper to bulldoze the place, then that's what I'm going to do."

"You can't."

"Watch me." He rolled up his window and backed out of the driveway.

Kara's heart was pumping so hard, her chest hurt, and when she looked down she saw that the check she'd written an hour earlier was now crumpled in her fist. She loosened her grip, folded it in two and carefully tucked it in her pocket. It was proof. Proof that she'd tried to pay on time—if this went to arbitration.

Since the storm, her mother and Wilma had been scouting the paper under the For Rent column of the classifieds. The only thing either of them could find in Kara's price range was located in Coos Bay.

Moving to another town would mean pulling the girls out of school and commuting daily along an often wet, winding stretch of road. She couldn't do it. And what would she do for day care? Leaving Esmeralda would break her daughters' hearts.

There has to be some other answer, she told herself, walking back to the damaged house. "Maybe I could pull an Uncle Kurt and chain myself to the front porch," she muttered. Morris couldn't very well bulldoze the place with her in it, could he?

Picturing their increasingly contentious relationship over the past year, she had a feeling the man might do just that—with glee.

Unless everybody in town was watching.

MONDAY MARKED JUSTIN'S first day back on the bus. Brad had gotten up early to fix him breakfast, which Justin had spurned in favor of a toaster bar. Life had more or less returned to normal in the week and a half since the storm, but Justin seemed intent on freezing Brad out. He never talked beyond a few obligatory grunts unless he needed something.

"Lunch money."

Brad could have offered to make him something,

but he didn't have the energy. He hadn't been sleeping well lately. Too many hot dreams filled with sweaty bodies—his and Kara's.

He walked to the calendar hanging beside the phone. A little sticker in the shape of a paw print was posted on the fifteenth. The day after Valentine's Day—one of the busiest nights of the year at Willowby's.

That reminded him. He needed to order roses. He gave a single rose to each of his female guests that night. It was a tradition Lynette had started, and he'd heard from many women who credited that flower with saving their marriage.

"My husband doesn't have a romantic bone in his body," one woman told him recently as she was making her February fourteenth reservation. "My Willowby's rose gets him off the hook."

He was just reaching for the phone when it rang. He glanced at the clock. Nine-fifteen. Couldn't be work. Too early. Besides, the restaurant was closed on Mondays and Tuesdays.

"Brad Ralston."

"Mr. Ralston, this is Officer Gomes with the Pine Harbor sheriff's department. We need you to come down and pick up your son."

"What happened?"

"Got in a pushing match with another kid as they were getting off the bus. The other kid hit his head when he fell. EMTs took him to the hospital for observation."

"Is he going to be okay?"

"Yeah, I think so. His parents are pretty upset though. Said your son has a reputation for being a bully. They wanted him to see the inside of a jail to teach him a lesson."

"I'll be right there. Do we need a lawyer?"

"Not at the moment. Might the next time this happens."

"There won't be a next time, Officer."

Brad hadn't stepped foot inside the sheriff's department since the last day of George's obedience school, which was taught by the town's lone K-9 officer. George and the other dogs had been required to hang out in the waiting room until the entire group was assembled. Lynette had begged Brad to take the giant pup to the Saturday morning classes because she'd been afraid she wouldn't be able to handle him around other dogs.

Brad had tried to be one of the last to arrive since his dog was by far the largest—and, he'd feared, the dumbest. But George had managed quite well. He'd learned enough to pass the course. And Brad had come to enjoy putting the animal through his paces. How had he forgotten that?

"Brad Ralston," he said through the window that separated the female officer at the desk from the dangerous civilians.

"Someone will be with you in a minute. Take a seat," she told him, her voice echoing hollowly through the low-tech speaker.

He turned around and started toward a grouping of chairs but found his path blocked by a man several inches shorter and fifty pounds heavier. "Ralston?" the man asked. "Your kid's Justin? The bully who attacked my son?"

"I haven't heard the whole story, but I'm very sorry your son was injured."

"Well, sorry ain't good enough. I want to know this won't happen again. I heard about your wife and all that. Divorce ain't easy on kids, but that's no reason for your boy to go off on my kid."

Brad agreed, but the man's contentious nature made him guard his reply. "Justin misses his mother."

"Yeah and from what my boy says, he's been hanging out with a rough crowd. Smokin' dope at your place after school."

That fear had crossed his mind earlier, but he hadn't seen any evidence that might indicate his son—or his son's friends—might be using drugs.

Brad was saved any further exchange with the man when the door opened and an officer motioned him forward. There was paperwork to fill out before he could see Justin. He signed on the dotted line, listened to yet another lecture on parenting and was given a brochure on anger management.

According to the contact information on the back of the flyer, a weekly group session was held at the community center on Wednesday nights. Parents and teens were encouraged to attend together.

Great, he thought sardonically, maybe I'll get my clone to take Justin.

When the officer who had been processing Justin's release left to get Justin, Brad sat on the hard, molded plastic chair, elbows on knees, absently trying to figure out what his options were. *Do I hire a live-in housekeeper? Could I afford one? Maybe Mom would...* The thought flew out of his head when he overheard an officer two desks away talking on the phone.

"Yeah, I know the place. Little blue house just off Hunter Street? Lost part of its roof in the last storm? What about it?"

Little blue house? That had to be Kara's place. Were she and the twins okay? Then he heard the man say, "Sitting on your front lawn with a sign because your landlord is a cheap SOB who won't fix your roof is not against the law."

Kara was taking on Morris Jakes? Was she aware that her unscrupulous slumlord had connections? His wife's brother was the chief of police.

The one-sided conversation continued. "How loud? Are we talking bullhorn or toy microphone?"

Brad sat forward, straining to hear.

"Listen, tell the guy who phoned this in—the landlord, right?—that it takes more than a boom box in the middle of the day to qualify as disturbing the peace."

The officer listened again. The look on his face changed to scornful. "Yeah, I know who he is," he said shortly. "But I'm due in court in fifteen. I'll leave a message for Vincente. He should be back within the hour. I'll have him swing by and check things out."

After the man hung up, Brad leaned over and tapped on his desk. "Excuse me. I couldn't help overhearing. That sounds like a friend of mine. Kara Williams. The dog groomer. Is she in trouble?"

The man, who appeared to be only a few years older than Brad, stood up. "I hope not. She's the only groomer we've ever had who can handle our hundred-pound lab." He put on his hat, readying himself to leave. "Apparently her landlord is trying to evict her on the grounds that the place is condemned. Black mold, he says. She disputes the claim and has set up a protest on her front lawn."

Black mold? After talking to the health inspector a week earlier, Brad knew how dangerous that could be. He also knew from driving by her house a time or two that the roof hadn't been repaired in the least. She was fighting for a piece of junk, which told him she didn't have any options. Rental property was hard to come by in this town—one reason Morris Jakes was rich and people like Kara were stuck in run-down buildings. If she had another place to go, she would never risk her daughters' health by staying in that hellhole.

Another place... An idea started to form. He needed someone to look after his son when he couldn't be there. Justin was too old for a nanny or a babysitter—and Brad was pretty sure they couldn't afford a housekeeper—but what if Brad invited Kara and her daughters to move into the guest wing?

Lynette had wanted the addition to house her family when they came to visit. As the fourth child—and first daughter—in a family of nine children, she'd made welcoming her parents and siblings, who mostly still lived near the family home in New Hampshire, a priority. Brad, an only child, had enjoyed his gregarious, fun-loving in-laws with their many offspring. Since the divorce, however, no one from Lynette's family had stopped by, much less stayed.

Trading that space for a bit of child care had never entered his mind. It probably wasn't an ideal solution given the fact this was a small town and people would talk—and he wasn't sure how Justin would react to the idea, especially after the incident at Willowby's—but it might just work. *If* he could convince Kara that his offer was totally above board. That what he was proposing was strictly platonic with no strings attached.

Which is exactly how he wanted to keep things between them. Wasn't it?

CHAPTER NINE

AFTER LEAVING THE police station, Brad took his son back to school. He met with Justin's principal while Justin talked to the guidance counselor. By then it was almost noon.

Thankfully, his son wasn't going to be charged with anything. Once the other students on the bus were interviewed, the verdict had been that both boys were equally responsible for the altercation.

The other boy's parents weren't happy, but they'd backed away from legal action. Probably, Brad decided, because their son had a smart mouth that had gotten him in trouble more than once in the past.

Justin would be allowed to return to class on the condition he attended a peer-counseling group that met daily at noon, as well as the Wednesday night anger-management class offered by Pine Harbor Social Services. Brad had been strongly urged to join his son at the evening sessions and he planned to try, but overcoming his scheduling challenges might depend on whether or not he was able to implement his new plan.

When he was on the phone with his lawyer, while waiting to meet with Justin's principal, he'd confided that he planned to ask "a woman" to move in as a sort of teen au pair.

"Does she know what she's signing up for?" his friend asked.

"I hope not," Brad replied, only half teasing. "But if the woman I have in mind agrees to do this, I think she's more than up to the task."

But first he had to run the idea past Justin.

He hung up as soon as he spotted Justin leaving the guidance office. "Walk me to the car."

Justin was clearly less than enthused about the idea, but he followed his father to the parking lot. "Get in. We need to talk. Don't worry. I'm not going to lecture you, but there's something I want to get your opinion on," he said before Justin could complain.

"Why did you bring George?" Justin asked, looking over the seat.

Brad glanced in the rearview mirror. "I'm trying to spend more time with him." George was sitting up, watching them. His eyes appeared filled with concern. Brad prayed he was doing the right thing. At least he knew this was a move George would endorse. If he could talk.

"Justin, we obviously need to make some changes. You're too old for a babysitter and too pissed off at the world to be left alone while I'm at work. We need help. You know how your mom always said things happen for a reason? Well, I don't know if that's true, but while I was at the police station this morning, I overheard an officer talking to someone about Kara."

"What'd she do?"

"Apparently her house has been condemned and her landlord is trying to evict her. She doesn't want to go even though the place is a piece of crap. I'm guessing that's because she either can't find a place in town or she can't afford what's available."

"So?"

"So, I got an idea. What if I ask her to move into the addition?"

"With the twins? No way."

"The only other option I can think of is to beg your grandmother to come."

Justin's belligerent look faltered. "Grams couldn't wait to get back to Arizona."

"I know. She likes her life there, but you're her grandson. She'd come if I made it clear you needed her. And, we have to face the facts, Justin. We need help."

"She…I…um… Dad, she's too much. She treats me like a baby. I can't…"

"She smothers you. I know. That's why I think Kara would be a better option. She's too busy to smother anyone." *And too kind.*

"Where would they sleep? There's only one bed in the addition." His suspicious tone implied he might have picked up on Brad's attraction to Kara.

"I figured Kara would probably want the girls to have the bedroom, and she'd sleep on the pullout bed. Your aunt and uncle slept there lots of times and never complained." He sighed. "Look, son, what I'm proposing is just a business arrangement. It would benefit Kara because it sounds like she really needs a place to stay, but it's really in our best interest—your best interest. Even though you might not see it that way at the moment."

Justin's body language appeared anything but receptive to the idea. "What about the twins? They'll get into my stuff. And they might paint George's toes again."

"They won't. I promise. And you have a lock on your door. They seem like very well-behaved little girls. I'm sure they'll respect your privacy if you ask them nicely."

He made sure to emphasize the last word. He didn't want any repeats of Justin's temper where Sophie and Sadie were concerned.

"Listen, pal, we're running out of options. You came this close to having a juvenile record today," Brad said, trying to stress the seriousness of his son's deeds. "You need to understand that every action has repercussions. What if that boy had gotten hurt really bad? Or, God forbid, died?"

Justin blanched—and for a moment he looked a very young fourteen. Brad reached out and grabbed his son's shoulder and gave it a squeeze. "This wild guy you've become lately—this hostile bully—isn't you, Justin. You're mad at me. At your mom. At everything that's happened. I don't blame you. This whole thing sucks. We can't change what has happened up till now, and I've been deluding myself that everything would miraculously go back to normal in time. We need help, son."

He could see that Justin wanted to argue, but a moment later a bell rang in the distance. Justin shrugged off Brad's hand and opened the door. "Whatever."

Brad watched him trudge back toward the building. He hadn't put up as much of a fight as Brad had expected. Maybe he understood at a gut level that something had to change. Brad hoped so. He also hoped his great plan would appeal to a certain dog groomer.

"So, George, what do say to bringing Kara and the twins home to live with us for a while?"

He turned in the seat to look at his dog. George stood up, his body filling the far back end of the Tahoe. His deep-voiced bark echoed off the windows. Brad nodded. "I'll take that as a yes. Let's go ask her."

His pulse jumped up a notch. Only because he was worried about her turning him down, right? God, he hoped that was why.

He turned the key in the ignition but stopped when a thought hit him. Morris might have caved in to Kara's public demonstration while all this business with the school had been taking place. He quickly pulled out his phone and called The Paws Spa. "Hi, Wilma, it's Brad. Is Kara there?"

"Nope. She's stuck at her house. Says she can't leave or Morris will swoop in and move all her stuff. It's supposed to rain again tonight and she doesn't have any way to get her things into storage. She could stay with her mother or me until she finds a new apartment, but neither of us has room for her furniture—what little there is."

Brad thought a moment. "Willowby's has a catering van that's sitting empty. I'll swing by and see if I can help."

"You better hurry. A friend called to tell me Morris was trying to get Kara arrested."

Brad doubted that would happen. The deputy at the station had seemed to be on Kara's side, but that officer wasn't the one who was going to investigate the situation. Truly, anything could happen when tempers were running high.

As he made his way out of the parking lot, he tried to picture Kara blowing her stack. Maybe if someone was hurting her daughters or a defenseless animal, she might get physical, but he really couldn't see it. Of course, he never would have imagined his son getting into a shoving match, either.

Until recently, Justin had been a mellow kid with lots of friends and an easygoing attitude. He played every type of sport—softball, soccer, water polo— and his coaches had always commended him on being a team player. But after his mother left, that child seemed to disappear.

Maybe having other people in the house would

provide a positive distraction. If Justin was worried about protecting his video games from the twins, he might not have time to stew over the fact his mother couldn't make room in her life to come see him or invite him for a vacation in Cancun.

Brad had tried to reach Lynette by phone several times to offer to pay their son's way to her place for spring break, but all he'd succeeded in doing was leaving messages with a service that *"no comprende ingles."* He didn't enjoy talking to her anyway because every conversation they'd had since the divorce wound up as just shouts and curses, but he was truly concerned about what her apparent abandonment was doing to their son.

Maybe having Kara's stable loving presence around would help bring Justin out of his present funk.

Brad stepped on the gas, suddenly feeling an urgency he'd ignored for too long. This could be a turning point for both him and his son. But first, he had to convince Kara that this was the right move for her, too.

KARA GOT UP from her lawn chair when a green and white four-wheel drive rolled to a stop in front of her house. The big gold star on the door and impressive rack of lights on the roof made her heart miss a beat. Morris had called the sheriff's department on her!

The officer behind the wheel didn't get out right away. She didn't know if this was standard intimidation protocol or if the guy really was talking on the phone, as he appeared to be doing.

Her first instinct was to run inside and lock the door, but she realized that was both cowardly and futile. Instead, she pulled her cell phone out of the pocket of her denim jacket and punched in the number of The Paws Spa.

"The cops just showed up. Promise me if I get arrested you'll keep the girls until I can raise bail?"

"Oh, Kara, that's not going to happen. You haven't broken the law."

The older woman's conviction helped relieve some of Kara's fear, but after the argument she'd had with her landlord that morning, Kara was afraid of what his next step might be. "Maybe I have and don't know it. Maybe Morris pulled some strings. He has connections, you know. Isn't his wife related to the mayor or somebody?"

"County sheriff, but from what I hear he's never been too fond of Morris—even before he turned into a slumlord."

Wilma's calm demeanor helped tamp down Kara's initial panic. But even if her friend was right—even if the policeman wasn't here to haul her off to jail—her life was in the toilet. She couldn't spend every day sitting on her front lawn, guarding her meager possessions and trying to convince her landlord not to evict her. She was losing money every minute—money she needed so she could find a new place to live.

Morris was right about one thing—her house was a hovel. Whether or not there was any dangerous mold, she didn't know. For once, she was actually sorry her mother's boyfriend wasn't around. Tony could have confirmed for her if there was a health hazard.

Mold or no mold, Kara did want to leave this sad wreck of a house behind. And she planned to—just as soon as she found another place. But being forced out this way—with little warning and the imminent threat of being arrested—was wrong.

Kara stood up a little straighter. She liked to think her uncle would have been proud of the way she was facing down a bully with too much money and no scruples. "I have to go, Wilma. The cop is getting out of his car. Keep your phone handy in case I only get one call."

"Don't call me. Call Brad Ralston. He's on his way there."

"Huh? What did you say? Why would Brad come here?"

"To help, I guess. He said something about a van."

Help? Kara's knees buckled. She might have staggered—which was definitely not the look she wanted to give the police—if not for her picket sign. She'd let it drop from its perch on her shoulder to lean against her hip while she was on the phone. Now, she used it to support her weight.

Brad was coming. Here. He'd somehow heard about her problem and was rushing to her rescue. Kara felt her cheeks flush with heat. Did this qualify as a swoon? she wondered.

Stop it, a voice in her head said sharply. *Brad's not a white knight. And I don't need him to be, anyway.*

She took a deep breath and tightened her hold on the old broom handle that she'd sawed in half to use for her sign post. She hoisted it to her shoulder and started pacing again, to the edge of the sidewalk and back.

She kept her chin high. She wasn't like her mother. She didn't need a man to rescue her. *What kind of role model would I be for my daughters if I turned into a simpering fool the moment Brad Ralston showed up?*

The sound of a car door slamming made her miss a step. She'd never been on the suspect end of a police investigation in her life. Her heart went into overdrive and her palms became clammy. The handle started to slip through her grip. She clutched it with both hands as the uniformed officer walked toward her.

He stopped a good eight feet away—presumably to be out of range if she tried to take a swing at him with her sign. Still, he was close enough for her to read his name tag: J. Vincente. He looked about thirty-five, but Kara didn't recognize him or his name. He would have been ahead of her in school, or he might be a new arrival. It was hard to tell much about him with his padded chest and reflective glasses.

"Is there a problem here, miss?"

"Y-yes." She hated the way her voice quivered.

She cleared her throat and tried again. "My landlord is trying to evict me without due process."

He took off his sunglasses and read her sign aloud: "'Show me the mold'?"

Kara thought she spotted a telltale flicker of humor around his lips. "My landlord says there's black mold. I say the claim is a ploy to get me out of the house so he can tear the place down and put up something that brings in more money."

"Did he give you a notice to vacate?"

"He says he doesn't have to because the recent storm that damaged the roof brought the problem to his attention and this is his only choice."

"But you want to stay here."

His tone was so judgmental Kara snapped. She let her sign dip toward the ground and took a step toward him. He instinctively tensed and dropped a hand toward his waist. Where his gun rested.

She froze and made herself take a deep breath. "Of course I don't want to stay here. I'm a mother. I have two little girls. Their bedroom was destroyed in the last storm and we've been showering at my business for the past week," she said as dispassionately as she could manage. "Look at this place. It's a cockroach-infested dump, but it's all I can afford at the moment. And Morris refuses to give me back my deposit because he says I kept animals here, which was against my lease."

"Did you?"

Tears filled her eyes. "A couple of bunnies and a

turtle. We're not talking fighting cocks or pitbulls, like some of his other renters."

The officer let out a sigh. She sensed that he wanted this to be settled quickly so he could go back to the station and tackle a "real" case. He was about to say something when a large white SUV came to a stop behind the patrol car. Brad jumped out, but before he could close the door, George cleared the distance from the very rear to the front seat and nearly mowed him over in his attempt to get out.

"Damn it, George. I said stay in the car."

George wriggled past Brad's valiant attempt to push him back. The dog jumped to the ground with a loud "umph" and loped to Kara's side, his tail wagging his entire back end. She smiled for the first time that day and let go of her sign to hug him. "Hello, my handsome friend. Are you here to rescue me from the big bad policeman?"

As if he understood her words, which she'd spoken jokingly, George turned to the deputy, making the man take a step backward.

Brad hurried toward them, greeting the officer with an outstretched hand. "Joe. Good to see you. How's everything?"

The two shook hands. Kara didn't catch the man's reply, but she heard Brad loud and clear. "What's it been—six months or better? I don't think I've seen you since the wedding. Not advisable, my friend," he said, shaking his head. "Just because you're married doesn't mean you can stop taking your wife out to dinner."

The policeman smiled—and looked a million times less intimidating. Kara actually started to relax, although she kept contact with George's neck for reassurance.

"Soon," Officer Vincente said. "Mandy keeps telling me we're going on a romantic date or else. And you know Willowby's is her favorite. I don't think she would've married me if I hadn't agreed to have you cater our wedding."

"A good woman with great taste," Brad said.

Kara thought that was laying it on a bit thick, but she kept her mouth shut.

Brad then directed the officer's attention her way, saying, "I see you've met Kara. Another good woman. Despite the fact she's carrying a protest sign. Or was," he added, walking closer to read the words Kara had written that morning using tempera paint on her daughters' poster board.

A big grin appeared on his face and he let out an appreciative chuckle. "Great sign, Kara. Direct, but not openly inflammatory. Morris would have a hell of a time suing you for defamation of character." He looked at Officer Vincente. "Especially considering what she *could* have written."

Kara wasn't sure what to say to that. She didn't even know why he was here, or if the policeman planned to arrest her, but before she could ask, Brad took another step closer, firmly aligning himself on her side, with George between them.

"Joe, I'm here to do you a favor. We both know

that protesting on your own lawn isn't a crime, and no matter what Morris says, no landlord can evict his tenant without going through the proper channels, right?"

The officer nodded fractionally.

"So, with Kara's okay, we can make this all go away."

"How?" she asked.

He didn't answer. His focus was still on the cop. "Come back in a couple of hours—wait, make it four—and everything should be back to normal."

"How?" Kara repeated.

The policeman looked as skeptical as Kara felt. "You're a cook and a diplomat?"

Brad laughed at that. "I'm a guy with a business proposition. One that hopefully Kara won't be able to pass up." He looked at her, and the pleading expression in his eyes made her third attempt at her question remain unasked.

He was winging this, she realized.

The officer shrugged, and then reached up to touch the microphone on his shoulder. Kara couldn't make out what he was saying, but George's ears quivered as if taking note of every word.

The cop left with a nod in their direction. "I'll be back around three."

Kara felt an instant reprieve as she watched the patrol car drive away, but mostly she was curious. "What's going on? What kind of business proposition?" she asked, bending over to pick up her sign.

George used the opportunity to lick her face.

She stood up too fast and was momentarily dizzy. Brad caught her arm and used the edge of his sleeve to wipe her cheek. "Sorry," he said. "Can we sit and talk a minute?"

He led her to the cluster of molded-plastic patio chairs she'd set under the leafless mulberry tree. Esmeralda had been over earlier with coffee and cookies, so there was a little table with paper cups, too. Kara sat down. George followed, sniffing around the grass, no doubt searching for crumbs.

Brad moved his chair so he was directly across from her. He leaned forward, resting his elbows on his knees. His hair was wind-tossed and in the bright light of day she could see a few silver strands beginning to show. His black, microfiber sports coat over a button-down white shirt made him look rather dressed up, but he was also wearing jeans and boots.

"Justin got in trouble this morning," he told her. "First day back on the bus and he and another kid got in a fight. The kid fell and hit his head. He wasn't hurt, thank God, but he could have been..." He didn't finish the thought. Kara had no problem filling in the blank.

"His guidance counselor and principal agree that Justin needs more supervision. Since this was his second offense on the bus, he might not be allowed to ride it for the rest of the school year. If that happens, I'll have to either make him walk every day or get up early enough to drive him."

He looked at his hands. "I guess I'm a bit naive. I thought walking to school would be good for him, but today I found out that he's been going just to the corner and catching a ride with some older kids. Boys that Lynette never liked and didn't want Justin associating with."

"Oh, that's bad news."

"I've been trying to wake up earlier, but on the nights I close, there's no way I'm fit to be behind the wheel at seven-thirty in the morning. My brain just doesn't work well enough after four hours of sleep."

Kara understood. She'd helped close Willowby's many times before she went away to college. After she got home on those nights, it would take her another hour or two to wind down enough to be able to fall asleep.

Brad wasn't done. "And, even if I do drive him to school every day, there's no way I can be home when school lets out. Right now, I try to take a break and check on him before the dinner rush, but, realistically, I can't be in two places at one time."

Kara nodded. She felt the same way where her daughters were concerned. Owning a business and being a single parent was like juggling bombs— every so often one blew up.

"So, what does that have to do with me?"

"As you know, I have a big house with a virtually empty addition. An addition big enough for you and your daughters."

"You want the girls and me to move in with you?"

"I need help, Kara. Justin needs…well, hell, he needs his mother, but I'm guessing that something isn't perfect in paradise because she hasn't been back to see Justin since she moved. Nor has she invited him down there for a visit. Either money is too tight or Reggie doesn't want Justin around. I don't know, but I do know my son is suffering for it."

"I don't blame him, but I still don't see…"

"You're a wonderful mother, Kara. Loving, involved. The way Lynette used to be. And even though you're not Justin's mother, I think he would benefit by being around you. I know your presence would provide a positive influence, and at the very least, you'd keep the negative influences from hanging around my house when I'm not there."

Kara was stunned, but she also believed in luck and timing. George had brought Brad into her life at a critical moment when Brad Ralston needed her help and she was out of options.

"Would I pay you rent?"

"I was thinking more along the lines of me paying you to take care of my son."

"Like a nanny?"

"No. He's not a baby, and you're a businesswoman—and the mother of twins. You already have two full-time jobs. I wouldn't expect you to clean or do our laundry or cook beyond what you'd do for yourself and the girls. The same cleaning crew that does Willowby's comes to my house once a week.

But I would want you to pick Justin up after school and make sure he stays home. Did I mention he's grounded for life?"

The last part was accompanied by a smile so she knew he was joking, but she liked that he'd made Justin accountable for his recent behavior. "It sounds like I'd have to change my business hours," she murmured, trying to picture how that would work.

"That's where my paying you comes in," he said quickly. "I wouldn't want this to be detrimental to you in any way. Bad enough you'd suddenly be in charge of a snarly teen. You can't lose money in the deal, too."

But she could see certain advantages for her that he might have overlooked. She'd save money on rent, utilities and several hours of day care. Less time spent at The Paws Spa would mean more time with her daughters. Two childhoods were slipping by so fast she was afraid to blink.

She rocked back in the wobbly chair and grinned. "This is sounding a bit like one of those Gothic novels Wilma is so fond of. You're Mr. Rochester and I'm the new housekeeper." She winked. "Thank goodness you don't have an attic. I really couldn't handle a crazy wife in the eaves."

"Don't worry. My crazy *ex*-wife lives several thousand miles away. Do we have a deal?"

He held out his hand.

She didn't hesitate, even though there were probably a million reasons why she should—beginning with the fact that she liked holding his hand. She made herself let go quickly and pet George, instead. "So, boy, are you in favor of this? The twins will try to ride on you."

George rolled his neck and shoulders, inviting her to scratch further down his back. His powerful tail made a loud swishing sound.

"Believe me, if George could talk, he'd be shouting, 'Yippee.' Haven't you noticed he's chosen you as his surrogate mother?" Brad stood up and rubbed his hands together as if eager to get going. "So. How much stuff do you have to move? We can load up the Tahoe, and then come back with my catering van."

She looked at the house. "Let's see. Some boxes of kitchen stuff. The twins' bunk beds have to go with us. And we have three dressers, although I've already packed all our clothes in plastic tubs since most everything had to be washed after the storm."

She glanced back at the SUV. "If we make a couple of trips, we might not even need the van. I'd planned to leave our lumpy old couch for Morris to deal with. The only really bulky thing is a table and four chairs that belonged to my grandmother. I think they'd fit in the back."

"Don't you have a bed?"

"I've been using a blow-up mattress, but I already took that to The Paws Spa…just in case Morris succeeded in getting me evicted today."

Brad seemed distressed to hear that she'd prepared for the worst-case scenario, but all he said was, "Then let's get moving."

Kara groaned. "Only if you promise no more bad puns."

He feigned hurt. "But they're the only kind I know."

The boyish expression on his too darn handsome face set off an alarm that brought with it a whole slew of new worries. Her bills might get paid, and she might finally find the time to start working on her franchise plan, but at what cost? What if her earlier crush came back? What if she fell in love with the man she and her daughters were about to be living with?

No, she told herself as she watched him walk up the steps of her sadly dilapidated house. That wouldn't happen. For one thing, she wasn't her mother. She'd never subjugate her own goals and ambition in order to have a man. Secondly, she was determined to be a positive role model for her daughters—especially in matters of love and life choices.

And then there was Justin. Brad's troubled son needed a friend and some stability in his home life. And that would never happen if his father started dating the nanny.

CHAPTER TEN

"IT'S TUESDAY, GEORGE. Hurry! We need to go over Justin's schedule for the week while Brad's home."

Kara couldn't believe she'd been living at Brad's for two weeks already. They'd survived Valentine's Day and a three-day weekend that had included Kara's first contact with Brad's former in-laws. Lynette's mother had called from Portland when Justin's train was late arriving. She'd been surprisingly pleasant, considering she was talking to the woman who was staying in the guest room her family usually occupied.

Justin had returned from his visit with his cousins and maternal grandparents a far mellower boy. For the past day and a half, he'd actually been civil to Kara and the girls, and he'd even smiled once or twice—when his father wasn't around.

It saddened Kara that Justin focused the majority of his ire on Brad, but she'd made every effort to keep her nose out of the Ralston men's business. Not that that was much of a challenge since Brad was rarely around. She could see how trying the restaurant business would have been on a marriage. She'd even found herself feeling a little sorry for Lynette, until she reminded herself that Lynette had worked along-side her husband for most of the years they were married.

She opened the back door of the garage and paused to remove her hiking boots and make sure George's feet were clean. One change she'd insisted on in her negotiations with Brad prior to moving in was that pets be allowed indoors. The bunny hutch had been transported from Kara's mother's house to a protected spot on the private patio beside Kara's bedroom, but the little thumpers visited inside often, and the girls had learned to use the vacuum after their pets were returned to their cage. Frida the turtle's terrarium occupied a spot of honor in the twins' room.

Kara had converted the main area of the guest quarters into her bedroom with shared family space focused around the TV and sofa. Once the pool table had been moved to the garage, there was a nice alcove for her bed. The openness didn't afford her a great deal of privacy, but she'd felt it was most important for the twins to have a place they could make their own. They'd managed to fill their room with pink frills, dolls and stuffed animals in a very short time.

And to her delight, the queen-size bed that had been in the guest bedroom was hers to sleep in, since the twins had their bunk beds. It had proven far more comfortable than her blow-up mattress.

George still slept in his kennel—unless it was stormy. Then he stayed in the pen during the day when everyone was gone, but once the family got home, George was welcome inside.

Together, they walked into the kitchen.

The smell of coffee brewing made her smile. She'd added her coffeemaker to the grouping of appliances on the marble counter. Not a huge contribution, but one that she and Brad enjoyed together on the mornings he joined them for breakfast. "Hi," she said. "Is Justin out of bed?"

Kara woke all three children before she left to walk George. So far, the twins had beaten Justin to the table every day.

Brad was seated at the far end of the island. He glanced up from the newspaper he was reading. She hadn't realized a man could look so incredibly sexy in a white T-shirt, ancient silk robe, sloppy pajama bottoms and bare feet.

"I heard the water running in his shower, so I assume so. I never expected it would be easier to get girls going in the morning than boys."

She grinned, giving in to the temptation to stare him up and down. "Whatever do you mean?"

One corner of his mouth pulled upward. A lazy, sleepy smile that made her insides do crazy flips. "Hey, this is my last day off. I'm entitled to a certain degree of slovenliness."

"I agree. And you do pull it off with panache."

"Thank you."

"You're welcome."

Their eyes met and for the length of a heartbeat—
or five—neither seemed able to look away. This connection had been growing more tangible ever since
Justin's trip. Nothing inappropriate had happened, of
course. No touching. No hint of impropriety. But the
fierce awareness between two living breathing adults
of the opposite sex was getting stronger.

And Kara didn't know what to do about it.

"What's for breakfast?"

Kara spun around, putting her back to the doorway where Justin was standing. She needed a moment to collect herself. She set down her mug with
a wobbly clatter and went to the refrigerator. "How
'bout a fruit smoothy and English muffins? I already
packed your lunch."

Justin uttered a grunt that she assumed meant
"Okay."

"You could say, 'Thank you, Kara, that sounds
lovely,'" Brad said. The gruff edge to his voice was
probably from sleep, but Kara knew Justin would
take it as criticism.

"Yeah, right," Justin muttered, sliding onto a stool
at the island.

Kara plopped the bag of muffins in front of him
and plugged in the toaster. She hadn't realized what
a pacifist she was until witnessing a couple of early
morning rows between the Ralston males. "Three,
please. Since you beat the girls out this morning,
you're in charge."

Brad seemed to take the hint and let the matter of his son's manners—or lack of them—drop. He returned to reading the paper.

A moment later, he let out a muffled exclamation. "You're running a St. Patrick's Day special?"

Kara stopped peeling the banana in her hand. "Yes. Remember when you told me that every holiday is a chance to give people an excuse to do something they might not normally do? Jeri, the high school girl who works two afternoons a week for me, suggested a St. Paddy's Day costume contest for pets."

To Justin, she said, "Do you think you'd like to bring George?"

Without a word spoken, the boy's face clearly said, "Only if you threaten my life."

"Shouldn't you be asking George?" Brad said, getting up to refill his coffee mug.

Hearing his name, the big dog left his sunny spot by the patio door and strolled into the kitchen. He looked at Kara expectantly. She dropped the banana peel into the compost container—another new addition to the household routine—and turned on the blender. "Sorry, boy, you don't like bananas. Prin does. Funniest thing I've ever seen."

Brad shook his head. "Who's Prin?"

"An old English sheepdog I groom. She'll eat a bite, roll it around in her mouth a minute then spit it out on the floor. Then she sniffs it for a while before she swallows it." She took George's head between her hands and leaned down to kiss his big black nose.

"Prin's show ring material but mentally challenged. Unlike this boy who is both smart *and* handsome. Like his father and brother," she added without thinking.

The moment the words were out she wanted to crawl under the dog and disappear.

Kara could feel Brad's gaze on her so she quickly stood up, washed her hands then poured the blender concoction into the three glasses she'd set out. "Sadie. Sophie. Breakfast," she called.

"Where's the butter?" Justin asked, his tone giving nothing away.

Kara reached for the covered dish the same instant Brad did. A classically awkward moment made worse by the fact his son was staring at them. Kara tugged the plate out of Brad's fingers and carried it to the island.

Her daughters provided a welcome diversion by noisily bursting into the room. "Justin," Sophie cried. "You're up."

"He beat us," Sadie complained.

Justin kept on buttering his English muffin as if neither had spoken.

"That's good," Sadie added. "Now, we won't be late for school."

"I don't make you late. You two are the ones who slow us down. You always have to kiss George and the stupid turtle before we go."

"And the bunnies," Sophie said, seemingly impervious to the boy's grouchiness. She climbed up on the stool beside him and picked up her glass.

Kara had always envied Sophie's attitude—part sweetheart, part "Bite-me." Sadie put as much room between her and Justin as possible. She kept her focus on the food, her feelings obviously having been hurt by the boy's accusation.

"Justin, apologize to Sadie," Brad said. "She's never made you late for school, and you know it."

Justin pushed his half-finished drink away and got up. "I'll be in the car."

Brad heaved a sigh and started after him. Impulsively, Kara grabbed his arm. "Attitude. I know. But I'd planned to drop the girls off first today, since we're early. How 'bout if I talk to him?"

"What set him off this morning? He's been a lot more pleasant lately."

Men could be so oblivious, she thought, somewhat gratefully. "It might be that he was hoping to hear from his mother by now. He told me you'd talked to his grandparents about the possibility of sending him for a visit."

Brad leaned his head against the frame of the door. There was something so defeated in his stance she couldn't stop herself from gently rubbing his back. "You can't fix this for him, Brad. It's between Justin and his mother. Trust me. I deal with mother issues every day."

She tried to make the last sound lighthearted, but a hint of pique must have given her away. He turned his head and said softly, "How did you become such a great mom when yours is…?"

"Wrapped up in her own life at the moment," she supplied, aware that her daughters were listening.

Between some kind of internal upheaval at work and the daily drive to Coos Bay to visit Tony, Nan seemed stretched to the limit lately. Her daily phone conversation with Kara—usually by cell phone as her mother was driving to or from the rehab center—had morphed into a sort of therapy session, with Nan sharing information about Tony's tragic childhood and speculating on how this might affect their future together. Rarely did she ask how Kara and the girls were doing, except in passing.

The sympathy in Brad's eyes was soothing. And inviting. A part of her wanted to slip into his embrace and let him shelter her from the reality of a mother whose world revolved around her boyfriend's dependency issues.

· But she couldn't. Plunging headlong into a relationship with a man who was recently divorced and on the rebound was exactly what Nan would have done. Kara refused to fall into that trap.

She stepped back, but not before the door opened again and Justin saw them. Standing too close. Kara's hand on his father's back. She didn't need a crystal ball to predict that their living arrangements were about to get more difficult.

BRAD POURED HIMSELF a second cup of coffee and walked to the patio door. He didn't go outside even though it looked like a beautiful morning. He inhaled deeply, savoring the scents of his new life: coffee, the ink from the newspaper on his fingers, the slightly repulsive smell of burnt bread crumbs from the bottom of the toaster. And something else. Something less easily identified.

Girl smells. Honeysuckle shampoo. Nail polish remover. Kara's perfume that followed him around like a genie tempting him to try his luck at three wishes.

He let out a sigh, which made George lift his head and look at him. Funny, Brad thought, inhaling again. He couldn't pick out any telltale clues that a dog lived in the house. Thanks to Kara's attentive grooming, no doubt.

He set his cup on the end table by the reading chair and went down on one knee. Taking George's head in his hands, he rubbed the base of the dog's ears, as he'd seen Kara do. George's eyes rolled back in the sockets and he moaned in bliss.

"You really are a good dog, George. You've liked having Kara and the girls here, haven't you?" He grinned. "Even if Sophie and Sadie try to dress you up like a doll."

George opened one eye. The effect was a sort of sardonic look that seemed to agree there were some things you did for love—even if they wound up making you look foolish.

Brad laughed out loud at George's expression and stood up. Motioning for the dog to follow, he walked through the kitchen toward the bedroom wing. The hall was wide enough for a decorative table Lynette had called her "seasonal altar." She'd rotate plants or dried flower arrangements beneath a collection of framed family photographs. Brad had been using the spot as a collection point for Justin's crap, and he noticed Kara had followed his lead. This morning she'd left a neatly folded pile of clothes on the table. A note was sticking out of the pocket. "'Morning, Mr. J. New T-shirt. S & S picked it out. Hope you like. K."

Brad examined the stack more closely. No mistaking the newness of the material compared to the worn and faded fabric of the others. "Good grief, George. Kara saw what I completely missed. My son needs clothes. Lynette always bought his things. It never even crossed my mind."

George nuzzled his hand.

Brad knew the dog was only trying to be petted, but the touch was comforting, just the same. It was like someone saying, "You can't know everything, man."

"Maybe I'll call Kara and tell her I'm picking Justin up after school. We'll drive to Coos Bay and do a little shopping."

He went to his room feeling a bit lighter of spirit. George followed at his heels. He stopped when he spotted a small white plastic grocery bag hanging from the doorknob. "Did I get a present, too?" he murmured, slipping it from the brass lever handle.

George leaned in and sniffed then backed up.

Brad grinned at the dog. "Does that mean it's not a bomb?"

He could tell by the bag that it came from the local grocery store. Inside, he found an open package of Post-it notes, a pair of tube socks—the kind with thick pads on the soles to help cushion his feet at work—and a Sudoku puzzle book. One of the yellow sticky notes was attached to the book.

"Knew the notes and socks were on your list. Thought I'd save you a trip to the store. The book is from the girls and me. Sadie said you were talking about trying the game. My tip: never guess at an answer. Enjoy, K."

"Wow. That was really nice," he said.

Suddenly, he felt terribly sad. He walked to the end of his king-size bed and sat. George followed, his tail wagging slowly as if picking up on Brad's abrupt downswing in mood.

"Lynette used to do this kind of thing—anticipate my needs without me even mentioning them." When exactly had that stopped? He couldn't pinpoint a day or even a year. There'd just come a time when Brad knew that he had to write down detailed lists if he wanted her to pick up anything for him. Most of the time, he shopped for himself, and let Lynette worry about Justin.

George laid his head on Brad's lap and stared up at him, his black brows knitted in a questioning look.

"If Reggie was here—and I still considered him my best friend—we'd be having this discussion, instead of you and me."

George's left brow shifted, as if insulted.

"Sorry, boy, but I'm not used to talking to a dog. I wonder if this is how Justin feels on the days he goes to the counselor—forced, one-sided communication." He sighed and pet the dog. "Truth is I'm a mess, George. I know that I need to stay focused on Justin and work. Period. I can't read anything into the nice little things Kara does for me. She's a sweet person. She's kind and thoughtful. Let's not forget that she's also really good to you. She walks you every morning, right?"

George lifted his head at the word *walk*.

Brad stroked the dog's thickly muscled neck. "There's a line that neither of us wants to cross." Well, he *wanted* to—God knew how badly he wanted to—but he didn't dare. "There's too much at stake. Things are working out pretty well considering we're two families living under one roof. There can't be any blurring of that line—new socks or no new socks."

He waved around the footwear to make his point. George's ear perked up, as if Brad were proposing a game of fetch.

"Do you want to play, George?"

He glanced out the window and smiled. "Why not? It's a beautiful day. To heck with paperwork."

He ripped off the label and broke the plastic tab

holding the socks together then pulled them on. Jumping to his feet, he gave George a satisfied nod and said, "Walk?"

The loud woof that followed seemed to echo in Brad's chest. The dog peeled out of the room, assumedly to get his leash. When Brad was dressed and had emerged from his walk-in closet, he found George sitting near the foot of his bed, tail wagging across the carpet like a windshield wiper. In his mouth was something small, gray and fuzzy. Definitely not a leash.

"Oh, God, George, tell me that isn't Floppy."

He held out his hand. "Drop it," he commanded.

George's jaw opened and he more or less spit the object into Brad's palm.

Brad gingerly held up a knitted hat. The stretched-out, bedraggled stocking cap Kara wore every morning when she took George for his walk.

Brad looked at his dog and snickered softly. "I don't know if you were intentionally telling me that Kara needs a new hat, but you're right. She does. I'll get Justin to help me pick one out when we go shopping this afternoon. You're a very smart dog, George. Now, let's walk."

Brad shoved the hat in the pocket of his windbreaker and started toward the garage. George trotted at his side, the jingle of his dog tags making a happy noise. Brad felt uplifted by the idea of buying Kara a little gift. Was he worried that she might read too much into the simple act of kindness? No, of course not. She'd done the same for him, hadn't she?

This was the first time since Lynette had left that Brad actually felt as though he was looking past his own needs and those of his son. He served the public every night at the restaurant, but that kind of focus was ingrained from years of professionalism. Thinking about someone else—a woman—and what it would take to make her happy—was totally different.

And he liked the feeling. A lot.

He'd just reached the door when the phone rang. A jolt of acid hit his stomach before he could scold himself for expecting the worst. Justin had been behaving himself at school and without the bus ride to contend with, there'd been no more incidents with his archenemy.

It rang again. He glanced at the clock. Eight-thirty. Too early for his mother to call.

He picked up the phone and checked the caller ID. It read: Out of area.

He looked at George, who was staring at the phone, not him. Finally, he depressed the talk button. "Hello?"

"Brad? It's me. Lynette."

CHAPTER ELEVEN

"BRAD? HI, IT'S ME. KARA. Can you do me a huge favor and get Justin after school? Wilma didn't come in to work today, and I'm worried about her. This is her regular Bridge day, but she's always here by two at the latest."

"Um…yeah, sure. Of course. Actually, I'd planned to pick him up anyway. I meant to call you. I thought I'd take him shopping for some new clothes."

Kara stopped brushing Banjo's sleek coat and adjusted her headset. There was an odd note in Brad's voice. Strained. "Is everything okay?"

He didn't answer right away, which made her stomach clench. She'd skipped lunch because of a drop-in. Kara had tried to explain that she was booked solid, but when the dog's owner said she'd come in response to the ad, Kara hadn't been able to say no. She'd told herself that even one new client would justify the expense, so how could she turn down that one new client?

Of course, at the time, she'd been counting on

her ever-reliable assistant to show up. *Wilma, where are you?*

"Yeah. Sure. Well…I just got off the phone with my attorney. Lynette called this morning."

"Really? Is she thinking about having Justin visit over spring break? That's coming up pretty fast, isn't it?"

He let out a weighty sigh. "Unfortunately, no. She wants to make a deal on the property settlement. If I'd sell the lot next door, she'd use the bulk of her share to settle with the IRS and pay off her debt to me. My lawyer is arguing that since we bought that lot with the money my father left me, I shouldn't have to sell it as part of the settlement."

"I didn't realize you had an option, but then I've never been through a divorce, so what do I know?"

"You know people. You know Justin. What do you think would be best for him? The lot is going to continue to go up in value. I figured I'd give it to him someday. He could build a house there if he wanted to stay in the area or sell it and use the money to build someplace else."

"Lucky kid. My uncle did that for me. He helped me buy this place, and believe me, without his backing, there's no way this business ever could have stayed afloat in the early months."

"Why can't Lynette understand that? I got the impression money is tight for her and Reggie right now. She said he's the head chef at a restaurant but, apparently, the wage scale is a joke. He can't return to the States because the IRS is on his case over some back taxes."

Kara helped the boxer off the grooming table and led him to a holding kennel. She still had two more animals to finish which meant she had to hurry if she was going to get the girls on time. As if hearing her concern, Brad said, "I'm sorry, Kara. This isn't your problem. With Wilma gone you're probably backed up. Do you want me to pick up the twins? We can kill some time at the park while you go check on Wilma."

"Really? You'd do that?" Kara had added Brad to her list of people who were allowed to pick up the girls from school shortly after moving into his house. He'd been the one to suggest it—"In case something comes up and you're late someday." Well, someday was here.

"Sure. Sadie won't be afraid to go with me, will she?"

"Are you kidding? The other day she was having a tea party while Sophie was watching TV with Justin. There were four spots and only two dolls. I asked her who else was coming and she said, 'I always save a spot for Brad. I know he's too busy to come, but my dollies think he's wonderful.'" I do, too, Kara had been tempted to add, but she'd managed to keep it to herself.

His earthy chuckle flowed through her body like a slow, loving touch. "That's sweet. I'll bring George along. I'm sure he'd enjoy a romp in the park. We were on our way out the door for a walk this morning when Lynette called."

Kara guessed the discussion must have gone poorly if Brad had felt the need to call his attorney right away.

"I'd better go," he said. "Don't want to be late for the girls. Call me and let me know what's up with Wilma."

"I will. Thanks. My next client is named Beauty. Unfortunately, she's anything but."

"Are we talking personality-wise or appearance?"

Kara glanced toward the waiting area and lowered her voice. "Wilma calls her a 'poodleaver.' Part poodle, part beaver. The dog's got teeth like you wouldn't believe, and she loves to use them. Fingers. Arms. You name it, she'll bite it. Wish me luck."

Brad's laugh brightened her mood. For a moment. But as she hung up, she sighed. He'd done as she asked and wished her luck. Too bad her foolish heart had heard a different L-word.

BRAD SAT ON THE PARK BENCH and watched the two blond beauties playing tag with his dog. As Kara had predicted, the girls had been delighted to see him—Sophie more so than Sadie, but even the shy twin's hesitation had vanished once she spotted George in the back of the SUV.

That had been over two hours ago. Kara should have called by now.

He pulled his phone from the clip on his belt and

checked the power. Full battery. A clear connection. He was about to flip it open and call her when it jingled.

"Kara? Is everything okay?"

"Brad? It's me. No. Everything is awful. I'm at the hospital. Wilma fell. The paramedics think her hip is broken. I found her at her house, almost passed out from the pain. The poor thing couldn't reach the phone to call for help."

Brad jumped to his feet. "Oh, my gosh, that's terrible. How long was she on the floor?"

"We don't know. She could barely talk. The EMT said she was suffering from shock, but that it could have been much worse if I hadn't gotten there when I did. I would have called you sooner, but one of her cats got out while they were loading the ambulance, so I had to find him for her before I came to the hospital."

"Are they doing surgery?"

"Probably eventually. The nurse I talked to said they needed to take X-rays and get her stable first. She's pretty out of it at the moment, but that's good because she was in a lot of pain. She's so strong and she hates for anyone to think of her as an old lady, but she was in agony when I arrived."

"How'd it happen?"

"I'm not sure. She might have tripped over one of her cats, but if you've ever been to her house…" She paused. "Let's just say it's a little cluttered. In a way, I'm surprised this hasn't happened before."

Brad liked Wilma. He didn't know her well, but

they'd talked a couple of times since Kara moved in with him. She struck him as the type who said what was on her mind and didn't pull any punches. "I'm so sorry. Do you want us to come to the hospital?"

She let out a long sigh that made him wish he could hold her and comfort her. "I ran outside to make this call, but I'm expecting Wilma's doctor to show up soon. She doesn't have any family, and I…" Her voice cracked. "I remember what it was like when my uncle was sick. A patient who is delirious with pain really can't make informed decisions. I think I should stay, but there's really nothing you and the kids can do at the moment."

Brad's father had died unexpectedly after a relatively routine surgery. No one could have predicted that a healthy seventy-two-year-old man would suddenly develop pneumonia and die forty-eight hours later. Even though he and his father had never been close, Brad still regretted not being at his bedside.

"Definitely. She needs you. Well, don't worry about a thing here. The girls are fine. We'll go order some flowers for Wilma then pick up Justin from school. If you don't mind, maybe we'll all go to the mall. Grab a bite at the food court."

She didn't answer right away. When she did, Brad could hear the emotion in her voice. "Sadie's dolls were right. You are wonderful. Thank you."

Three hours later, Brad felt anything but wonderful. His grand plan was turning into a grand disaster. Justin hadn't been overjoyed by the prospect of going anywhere with two little girls, but once Brad explained the situation with Wilma, at least he'd settled into his seat and stopped complaining.

The actual shopping part of the adventure turned out to be fairly simple. Justin didn't like anything Brad suggested, so Brad and the twins made a game of guessing what Justin would choose. Sadie, it turned out, knew the young boy's taste better than either Brad or her sister.

"He'll pick the army-green shirt," she'd said, peering in the window of the trendy-looking store where Justin had disappeared moments earlier. "And those pants with the chains on them."

Brad had been prepared to nix anything with chains, but when Justin emerged from the dressing room wearing exactly what Sadie had predicted, he'd swallowed his objection. The clothes made his son look older, but there was something about the way Justin walked with shoulders upright instead of his usual slouch that sealed the deal. And the chain appeared to be sewn to the belt loops. Surely that kept it from being a potential weapon, right?

To be fair, Brad also offered to buy the twins a couple of things. After a quick huddle, they agreed that their mother would probably be okay with one small gift apiece. He accompanied them to a children's boutique while Justin played video games.

Watching them ooh and ahh over the bright, surprisingly pricy outfits was about the most fun Brad had had in months. They were not only beautiful but thrifty. Both girls reflected their mother's influence by choosing moderately priced tops—matching designs, although one in pink, the other purple. Both were dotted with sparkles, which seemed to make them very happy.

After he paid for the purchase, Sophie hugged him. "We'll wear these to school tomorrow. Thank you very much, Brad. You're nice." Sadie nodded with fervor but didn't step close enough to hug.

"You're welcome. Who's ready for dinner?"

"I am."

"Me, too."

"Good. But first, let's run these bags to the car and check on George. He'd probably like to stretch his legs," Brad said, thankful for the mild temperature that made it possible to leave the dog in the car without worry.

They returned a few minutes later to pry Justin away from the loud and violent-looking game he was playing. Fortunately they were early enough to find seats in the food court. Justin insisted on Mexican food. The girls didn't seem to care, so Brad ordered a variety of choices along with four drinks and carried the tray to the table—just in time to hear Sophie reprimand his son.

"You're not nice too much of the time. And if you don't stop being mean, we're not going to like you anymore even if you are a kinda brother."

Justin's brows—so like his mother's—created a V above his nose. "I'm not your brother."

"I said kinda. Like Bethany Riggs. Her older brother is adopted, and when her mom married Mr. Riggs, she got two kinda sisters…and a deaf dog."

"Mommy says the dog isn't really deaf but it won't listen to anybody—even Mommy—so it might as well be," Sadie added.

Justin didn't reply. Brad couldn't tell if that was because he was stunned by the well-developed argument—from a five-year-old—or because he was trying not to smile. He wouldn't make eye contact with his father so Brad didn't know for sure.

"Food," Brad said lamely.

The twins took napkins and forks before picking out an entrée from the oil-slick wrappers. Bean and cheese burritos. He wasn't surprised.

Justin grabbed four items without bothering to read the labels. That left Brad with either a chimichanga or an enchilada. He took the latter.

They ate in silence, although the twins seemed to communicate without words. As Brad had detected from the breakfasts they'd shared over the past weeks, Sophie devoured her food with gusto while Sadie ate slowly with ladylike grace.

"Can I go back and play some more video games?" Justin asked, crumpling his trash into a big greasy ball.

Brad shook his head. "I promised the girls they could hang out at the play area for a few minutes. It's on the way to the car."

Brad had another reason for wanting time alone

with his son while the twins played. He'd decided Justin needed to know about Lynette's call. If he waited until they got home, Justin would storm off and lock his door. In public, the two might actually get in some dialogue.

Ten minutes later, with the girls occupied, Brad turned to Justin, who was sitting a foot away, and said, "Your mom called this morning."

"Did you talk about me going to see her?"

"Air travel is really expensive right now. And Cancun is a big destination spot for college kids on spring break. We both felt the timing wasn't right." The excuse Brad came up with because he'd known Justin would ask. "The main reason she called was to tell us that she and Reggie set a date to get married. And to talk about the property settlement."

"You said the divorce was final."

"It is, but we still haven't worked out all the details on things like the lot next door."

"When's the wedding?"

"Um…June second, I think she said."

"Can I go?"

No. Because your mother doesn't want to see you until after she's got a ring on her boyfriend's finger. "I don't know. We'll see."

Justin's eyes narrowed. "You don't want me to go, do you? You're always going to have some excuse why I can't go. You want to punish Mom for falling in love with Reggie by keeping me here."

Brad bristled. "That isn't true, son. Honestly, we

didn't talk about her wedding plans. I don't have any idea what kind of wedding she's having, but if family is invited, I'll do my best to make sure you're there. Mostly, we talked about whether or not I should sell the lot next door."

"Are you going to?"

"I don't know. I have an appointment with my accountant tomorrow. I don't *want* to. I like not having neighbors up close and personal, but I might have to get some closure." *Lynette's word.*

"Why? So you can marry Kara?"

Brad's pulse spiked. "What?"

"I saw the way you looked at her this morning. And now you're out doing the daddy thing with her kids."

Brad shook his head. "I'm helping with the twins because Wilma fell. I told you that."

Justin jumped to his feet. "Well, just so you know, we'll never be one big happy family. *My* family doesn't exist anymore. And those twins aren't my sorta sisters and never will be." He put out his hand, palm-up. "I wanna wait in the car."

Brad decided to let the subject drop. He'd known there was some risk in having Kara move in because he did like her—and in the past weeks his feelings had grown. What that meant he wasn't sure, but he knew he couldn't cram another change down his son's throat. "Fine. Take George for a walk. Just don't go too far. We won't be long."

As he watched his son walk away, he recalled

Lynette's response to his accusation that she'd abandoned her son. "Don't say that," she'd cried. "I'm building a new life here. A good life filled with mutual love and respect. I plan for Justin to be a part of that, but I can't make it happen overnight."

"And in the meantime? Justin needs more than your occasional long-distance call, Lynette. He needs a mother."

She'd started sniffling then. "Is that why Kara Williams moved in? To take my place?"

Brad had known the subject would come up, eventually. "Kara *and* her five-year-old twins are staying in the addition," he'd said pointedly. "One of the reasons they're here is because our son sent another child to the hospital after an altercation on the bus. Justin's principal basically told me to get help or our son would be kicked out of school. I have a business to run, Lynn, and since my partner is gone and I can't be two places at once, what choice did I have?"

Lynette was quiet a moment, then she said, "I always liked Kara. She's a hard worker." Her words sounded like a peace offering.

"Her rental house was damaged in a storm, and this worked out for her, too. She's good with Justin. Patient, but doesn't let him walk all over her."

"Is there something romantic between you two?"

"Do you have any right to ask?"

"I guess not, but one of the reasons Reggie and I are holding off on having Justin visit is we both feel we should be married before he comes. We don't want him to see us living in sin."

Brad còuld have—might have—said something snide, but the operator had broken into the call to tell Lynette she needed to deposit more money.

"I have to go, Brad. I'm sorry about everything. I'll try to call Justin more often. I wish I had regular e-mail but we don't have a phone line at our place. That's something I plan to get as soon as you sell the lot and give me my share."

Lynette's call had left him feeling both frustrated and confused. Was he hurting his son by not giving in on the property settlement? Or would Reggie—ever the big spender—just blow the money? Despite the promise of upcoming nuptials, Brad had gotten the impression his ex-wife and his ex-best friend were struggling to make their relationship work.

That should have made him happy, but, oddly, it didn't.

He stood up and called for the twins. They immediately dashed to his side.

"Where's Justin?"

"He went to the car to walk George before the long drive home." At least he hoped dog, boy and car would still be in the parking lot when they got there. "But I need your help before we leave. See that accessories shop over there? Do you think we can find your mother a new hat if we try?"

Their matching smiles were almost enough to

ease the pain of knowing his son's heart was aching. Almost. What helped the most was knowing Kara would be at the house when they returned.

CHAPTER TWELVE

"How's Wilma?"

Kara was so tired she could barely move, but she'd made herself return to the living room after changing clothes and showering because she knew Brad would be waiting to hear about the events of her day.

"The break was worse than they thought. The hip is a fairly common injury with women Wilma's age, but apparently she also fractured her pelvis. They think she must have hit a piece of furniture as she fell." She sat down on the soft leather sofa a foot or so away from him so they could talk without being overheard. She knew the twins adored Wilma, and she'd tried to keep the prognosis fairly upbeat when she told them about Wilma's condition.

The twins had been too keyed up to go to sleep after their big outing, of course. She'd read them three books before finally turning out the light and ordering them to be quiet.

Where was her patience? Oh, right, she thought dryly, it got lost while tracking down that disagreeable cat of Wilma's. She picked at the edge of the adhesive bandage she'd stuck on the back of her hand after she'd finally caught the beast.

"Wilma doesn't remember what happened?"

"Not exactly. I love her dearly, but the woman is the worst pack rat I've ever known."

She closed her eyes, picturing the mess. "She said she was in a hurry because she didn't want to be late for work. That, of course, made me feel guilty for depending on her so much."

"Kara, she loves working for you or she wouldn't do it. Besides, I can't imagine her doing any differently if she worked at Wal-Mart or any other place that hires older workers."

His support was a welcome balm.

He stood up. "You need a nightcap."

He was out of the room before she could stop him. Alcohol might push her right into an emotional breakdown. She'd called her mother while Wilma was getting an MRI. "Face it, Kara. Wilma's getting up there in years. You should feel grateful this didn't happen at work. Your insurance would have dropped you like a hot potato if they'd had to pay out that kind of claim."

Kara wanted to think her mother was trying to find a bright side of things for her daughter's benefit, but Nan's lack of empathy had really gotten to her.

Maybe if Mom had come to the hospital and seen Wilma, she would have been more sympathetic, she thought. Propped up with pillows under her back and side, her friend had looked so fragile and bewildered.

Kara let out an involuntary moan. That was all it took for George to plop his head on her lap.

"Oh. Hello, boy," she said, petting him effusively. "Did you have a good day? The girls talked nonstop about how you played with them at the park."

"We had a great day...until George got car sick," Brad said, handing her a glass filled with a layer of brown liquid topped with a layer of white. "Kahlúa and milk over ice. I don't usually have alcohol in the house, but this came in a holiday basket from my staff."

She accepted the offering, suddenly craving something sweet and chocolaty. She used the plastic stir stick to mix the two layers until the color turned pale umber. She closed her eyes and took a sip. "Yummy. Thanks."

"You're welcome. Now, tell me the prognosis."

"They'll do surgery in the morning. As soon as she's able, they'll move her to rehab. After that, who knows?"

"What do you mean?"

Kara blinked back tears. "One of the nurses said Wilma might need to use a walker for the rest of her life. Her doctor made it sound like she'd have to move into a senior facility that could help care for her. Permanently."

Brad leaned forward slightly, reaching past her to

stroke George's neck. "What's wrong with that? Wouldn't she be better off in town rather than all alone on a farm in the country?"

Kara took a big swallow of her drink. "She says those places are for old people. This might kill her spirit."

His broad shoulders lifted and fell. "I don't mean to sound flippant, but there's a reason they call those places 'independent living.' My mom moved into a really nice one about six months after my dad died. I tried to convince her to stay with us—at least at first, but she was adamant about standing on her own two feet. She's been very happy there."

"Did I tell you she called the other evening to talk to Justin? She seems nice. Very warm and friendly."

"She is. And smart. She and Lynette probably would have ended up killing each other if she'd moved here. Mom's no fool. She'd have picked up on Lynette's cheating right away."

Kara thought that was a funny thing to say. "What makes you so sure? You're no fool and you didn't know."

He shifted positions, pulling one knee up on the cushion. She knew he didn't like to talk about his marriage and his friend's betrayal, but Kara couldn't understand why he readily accepted so much of the blame for what happened.

"The signs were there. I chose to ignore them."

"What kind of signs?"

He glanced at her and smiled. "She stopped buying me new socks when the old ones wore out."

Kara pretended to gasp. "Oh, my God. Not that."

He chuckled softly. "There were other things, too. Little things. Inconsequential by themselves, but in hindsight they definitely constituted a pattern—if I'd been paying attention."

Before she could say anything, he added, "Even though we're just housemates, of sorts, you've done more wifely gestures in the past few weeks than Lynette did in the last few years of our marriage."

Kara frowned, swirling the ice in her glass. "Wifely? I don't think I like that word. It makes being married sound like a job."

"Believe me, it felt like one at the end."

"Did you perform your husbandly duties?" She realized that wasn't the question she'd intended to ask the moment the words left her mouth. Just how much booze was in her drink? "Wait. That came out wrong."

"You want to know whether or not I was being attentive to Lynette's needs during that same time period? The answer is probably not. We were in the process of being audited. I was so focused on saving my business I didn't see what was going on in my life."

He sounded as though he truly regretted his mistakes. She reached out and touched his forearm. "Wilma told me when I was leaving tonight not to fret because things happen for a reason." She blew out a sigh. "Why do people always say that after something bad happens?"

"Maybe because the bad thing is actually good but you're too upset to know it at the time."

"Huh?"

"I don't mean that Wilma's broken hip is good. That's going to change her life, but something good could come of it. Maybe she'll move into the retirement home, meet some nice guy and wind up—"

"Falling in love?" she blurted out.

He tapped her nose. "I was going to say, 'with a close friend to keep her busy and involved for the rest of her life.' Like Andrew. The man my mother is seeing. She refuses to call him a boyfriend, but they do a lot of fun things together.

"Dad's death was really hard on her, but she's doing things now my father never would have considered trying—like zipping around the lake on a Wave Runner."

Kara tried to apply what he was saying to Wilma, but the image just wouldn't materialize. Not just the part with Wilma on a Jet Ski, but Kara couldn't picture Wilma dating. She was too…cranky. Like her cats.

Her cats. "Damn," she mumbled. "I forgot to go back to the farm and feed the cats and give them their medication."

Brad checked his watch. "Well, you're not going anywhere tonight. You've had a drink and you're exhausted."

She knew he was right, and even though she didn't like anyone telling her she couldn't do something, having that option taken off the board was a relief. "I'll do it in the morning after I drop off the kids. One night won't kill them, but I feel bad. They're probably lonely without Wilma."

Brad made a funny sound and reached out to touch her cheek. "You're the kindest person I've ever known. Wilma and I are both lucky to have you in our lives."

He scooted closer to give her a hug.

His warmth and solidness were a refuge from the grueling hell of her day. It was nice to be appreciated. She settled into the crook of his arm as if she belonged there. As if they were an old married couple who knew exactly how to comfort each other.

Brad didn't mean for his gesture to be anything more than a show of support but once she relaxed against him, he found he couldn't let go. She was so strong, and yet so fragile. She gave so much of herself to him, to his son, to her daughters…even to a couple of unfriendly cats at her best friend's house.

During the weeks leading up to his separation from Lynette, she had accused him of being self-absorbed and greedy. "You never contribute anything but money to this family," she'd told him.

Money that she had used to buy anything and everything she needed to be fulfilled. Wasn't that what good husbands did? That's what his father had done—until he died.

After his father's funeral, he remembered, his mother had been thumbing through the photo albums she'd set aside to give Brad and said, "We never appear to be smiling in these pictures. Do you think your father was ever happy?"

Lynette had turned the question on him during the flight home. "What about you, Brad? Do you like your life?"

"Of course," he'd answered without thinking, but since that time he'd had innumerable reasons to reconsider.

"Kara," he whispered against her hair, "are you happy?"

"Hmmm?" she answered, her face turned toward his chest, eyes closed.

He slipped the glass from her loose hold and set it on the table just behind her. The movement brought them closer together. Kara's sleepy body didn't protest or push him away. In fact, she looped her arms over his shoulders and snuggled closer.

The rise and fall of her breath pushed her breasts against him. She was the first woman he'd held like this since long before his divorce. There'd been plenty of hugs from the women in his life and even a couple of propositions, but nothing quite this intimate. He could smell a faint hint of alcohol from the tiny bit of Kahlúa he'd put in the drink.

He didn't plan to kiss her, but when she stretched in a half-awake way, her eyelashes fluttering against her cheekbones, he couldn't help himself. *Just a taste.*

But one taste turned into two, and the sparks of attraction they'd both been ignoring ever since that first afternoon in the parking lot of The Paws Spa ignited.

Her mouth relaxed and her tongue welcomed him with a little exploration of its own. He couldn't contain the low groan of pleasure.

The sound must have reached George because the dog suddenly sat up and barked. The rumble of a Great Dane's voice can be startling even when you're braced for it, but when it bursts forth with no warning…

Kara's eyes flew open and she jerked back. A bright red blush filled her cheeks as she clapped a hand over her mouth. "Oh, no," she said, stumbling to her feet. "I'm so sorry."

"Why?" Brad asked, giving his dog a severe look. George dropped his head in shame. "It was just a kiss."

"But we agreed no hanky-panky."

"No what? That sounds like something Wilma would say."

"She did. Before I moved in here. She said I needed to keep my distance—physically and emotionally."

Ten minutes earlier Brad would have agreed. "Why? We're both adults. And single."

She staggered backward, narrowly missing George's paw. "No, we're not. We're both package deals. Kids. Pets. Demanding businesses. Baggage," she added meaningfully. "Brad, I'll be honest. I've had a crush on you ever since I waited tables at Willowby's, but I'm not going to fall in love with you. I can't let myself."

Good, he almost said. He should have said. But instead, he asked, "Why?"

"Because you're still getting over Lynette. You talked to her this morning and look what happens tonight—you wind up kissing me."

Brad wanted to point out the flaw in her logic, but she didn't give him a chance. "I lived through a rebound relationship with my mother. She married a man too soon after my father died. She was in pain, and she wasn't thinking straight. We both paid the price."

Brad wasn't sure what that meant, but he could tell even the memory was distressing to her. "I'm not saying you're anything like Doug. You're not. But this is too soon. For you, and more importantly for Justin. Maybe I shouldn't stay here."

That made Brad rake his hand through his hair. "Kara, you're exhausted. That kiss wasn't going anywhere. We both needed a little comfort. I'm sorry it shook you up, but don't overreact."

She started to say something but stopped. Without another word, she left the room.

Brad had no idea what would happen in the morning. Lynette always had to have the last word when they argued. He just hoped Kara would believe him and stay. Even though he knew he'd been lying through his teeth. If George hadn't interrupted them, who knows how far that kiss would have taken them. Maybe to paradise.

CHAPTER THIRTEEN

"HEY, LAZY BONES," Kara called as she and George walked in the door of Wilma's room at the Sunny Vista Rehabilitation Center. "My friend here wants to know when you're going to get off your tush and come back to work."

Kara had been to the facility every day since Wilma's transfer from the hospital, but this was the first dog-approved visit.

Wilma was sitting in a wheelchair by the window working on some kind of puzzle book. She looked up—her short silver hair sticking out at odd angles like a broken halo. "'Bout time you got here, George," she said, ignoring Kara completely. "Come give me a big slobbery kiss. I told all my rehab friends about you. Told them you're a real gentleman, so don't make me eat my words by peeing on anything."

Kara laughed and led the dog closer so Wilma could lean over and give him a hug. She had to bite on her lip to keep from crying. Seeing Wilma in a wheelchair was hard enough but knowing her friend's chipper attitude was put on for her benefit made her sick at heart.

Wilma was worried about the future, about becoming dependent on others and being alone. The nurses had confided some of Wilma's concerns to Kara, assuming, she guessed, that Kara was Wilma's daughter. Kara wished she were. Her real mother hadn't been available—emotionally or any other way—since this crisis began.

Kara knew why, of course. Tony. Apparently he'd reached some kind of wall in his therapy and was threatening to check himself out.

Big deal, Kara had wanted to scream. But she didn't. She half listened to her mother's worries, while in the back of her mind, toying with the idea of moving in with Nan if Tony took off. The mobile home just wasn't big enough for all of them—especially if Tony started drinking again.

But Kara needed something in her life to change. Every day was a kind of torture for her. Seeing Brad, wanting him, knowing she couldn't touch. Her libido had switched from the ascetic monk setting to wanton nymphomaniac with just one kiss. And a fairly platonic kiss at that. Who knew what would have happened if Brad had really kissed her? Hard. With passion and desire equaling hers.

"You're not coming down with anything, are you?" Wilma asked. "You look a little flushed."

"I'm fine."

"Sure you are. Have a seat and tell me about it.

Is it that new helper you've got taking my place? I knew she wouldn't work out."

Kara sat on the end of the bed. Wilma was talking about Claudia Mosely, Brad's evening hostess at Willowby's. He'd overheard Claudia telling another employee how empty her life was with her children out of the house. She'd been considering getting another part-time job to keep busy.

He'd immediately suggested she contact Kara.

"Why is that?" Kara asked Wilma.

"She's a people person. Deals with the public every night at the restaurant. Smiles a lot. Believe me, dogs and cats can tell when they're being patronized."

Kara tried to keep her tone free of humor. "I see. Well, maybe she's part animal person, too. Did you know she's involved with the greyhound rescue program? She has three retired racers and a Chihuahua."

Wilma's already pensive look turned sour. Kara could guess what she was thinking—that there wouldn't be a place for her at The Paws Spa once she was well.

"Claudia is doing fine. She loves it and is thinking about cutting back her hours at Willowby's to work for me every day."

"You're giving her my job?"

"Yes. And I'm giving you *my* job."

"What?"

"You know my dream is to create a Paws Spa

franchise operation. Well, I can't do all the legwork that involves while I'm grooming dogs forty hours each week. All of my business books say you've got to spend money to make money. So, once you're back on your feet, I'd like you and Claudia to work together so I can get my expansion plan under way."

Wilma thought a moment then said, "Are you sure you're not jumping the gun with this? Maybe you should wait till the twins are in school."

"In the fall, they will be. If I wait too long, someone else will do it. Next thing you know, financial wizards will be talking about the Starbucks-of-pet-grooming, and it won't be my Paws Spa they're referring to."

Her friend leaned over and spoke into George's ear. "She's not telling me everything. She thinks because I'm old and infirmed that I can't tell she's upset about something, but we know, don't we, George?"

Kara started to scoff at the idea, but George looked at her solemnly as if agreeing with Wilma. The compassion in his eyes was her undoing. She slumped forward, dropping her face into her hands. "I'm a mess. I'm trying to stay focused on the future because the present is too mixed up."

Wilma rolled her wheelchair a couple of inches closer. "Kara, what's wrong? This isn't like you at all. You're strong and fearless."

Kara shook her head. "I just discovered that I am my mother's daughter," she cried.

"In what sense?"

"I'm having the wrong kind of dreams about Brad."

"And Nan is, too?"

Kara smiled, as she knew was her friend's goal. "He might be the only recently single man she hasn't dated."

"Oh," Wilma said sagely. "It's the timing of these dreams that is bothering you. Brad and Lynette haven't been divorced for all that long."

Kara rubbed her temple. She'd done the math—a dozen times since that night when they'd kissed. Every brain cell had screamed, "Too soon."

"That's part of it. I'm not sure he's really over her." He'd made very few changes to the house to indicate he was ready for a fresh start. Lynette's voice was still on Willowby's answering machine, for heaven's sake.

Wilma's face scrunched up in thought. "I used to know a quote by Helen Keller. I can't recall the exact words at the moment, but it's something about life either being a great adventure or nothing at all. There's risk in just getting up in the morning, Kara."

"I know what it's like to be left, Wilma. You were there. You know what an emotional basket case I was for a good year after Fly took off."

Wilma's frown turned tender. "These darn drugs have been messing with my memory, but I can picture you crying over a poopy diaper. Did that happen?"

"Yes, but it wasn't just any diaper. That was the last one. I'd put it on Sophie a minute earlier and didn't have enough money to buy more."

"So I showed you how to improvise by cutting up layers of an old flannel shirt."

Kara smiled, recalling the image of her plaid-bottomed infant. "But the point is nobody but you and my family dared to be around me. And I certainly wasn't in any shape to make life-altering decisions." *Like falling in love.*

"Did it ever occur to you that your emotional state had very little to do with Fly leaving and everything to do with your being a new mom?"

"No, not really. But what about Nan? She married Doug less than three months after Dad died and look how badly that turned out." Kara hadn't shared her harrowing story of living under the thumb of her mother's biggest mistake with many people, but Wilma knew.

"I'll admit your mother jumped into that frying pan without looking, but she's always regretted it."

"Yeah, but did she learn from her mistake? No. Every time a boyfriend breaks up with her, she vows she's going to give up men for at least a year." Kara heaved a long, deep sigh. "Tony showed up not two weeks after Jack the Rat left with Mom's new flat-screen TV."

Neither spoke for a moment. George, obviously bored with the conversation, sank to the floor and closed his eyes.

"Even if I agreed with you about your mother, you're overlooking one very important difference—you. How long has it been since you've gone on a date? You make me look like a wild woman."

Kara snickered. They both knew Wilma hadn't been on a date since her husband had passed away. "I wasn't thinking about me so much as Brad."

"Oh. Maybe healing time is different for men. What does he say about this?"

"Nothing. I mean we haven't discussed it. We're sorta pretending nothing happened."

"Something happened?" Her friend's loud bark startled George, who let out a yip and looked around.

"A kiss. A little one. But…I've always had a bit of a crush on him. And now that we're living in the same house, I can see what an amazing man he is. A great father—even if Justin doesn't think so. And speaking of Justin, that's another whole can of worms. Big, slippery, emotional ones."

"The boy's mad about his mother leaving and needs someone to blame," Wilma said, sizing up the problem quite succinctly. "And Brad is handy."

For never having had children, she could be quite astute about divining what motivated them, Kara thought. "I agree, but even though Justin is angry at his father, he probably still hopes his parents will get back together. Most children of divorce do—or so Claudia said. She's a big Dr. Phil fan."

"So, you think if he found out that you and his dad were interested in each other…"

"It would be like tossing a lit match on a container of gasoline."

In the quiet that followed her statement, Kara could hear a steady hum of phones ringing and intercom calls for "nurse so-and-so." The constant noise reminded her of working at Willowby's. Only, the smell wasn't as inviting.

"You know, I might be able to help you move out of Brad's, but I feel guilty even suggesting it."

"Why?"

Kara listened as Wilma explained what her doctor had told her earlier that morning. Wilma was making excellent progress in her therapy. He was ready to release her to an out-patient program but only if she had help at home.

"Especially at night," Wilma said. "I'm no pauper. I can afford to hire a nurse, but that means bringing in a stranger. The cats wouldn't like that." She brightened. "How are they?"

Kara looked at the scab on the tip of her thumb, which was still healing from her last lesson in wildcat etiquette. Rule number one: never touch Pooka when he's eating. "Fine, I guess. They don't actually let me close enough to know for sure, but their food is gone in the morning when I show up. I only have a few scars from trying to get Pooka to take his pills."

Wilma smiled. "They miss me."

Tell me about it.

"So, maybe you and the twins could move in with

me. I know Brad would be disappointed, but it might save him grief in the long run."

And what would it save Kara? Heartbreak? Or unrivaled happiness?

"I can't leave Brad high and dry. I owe him better. He rescued us when Morris was trying to evict me. Maybe if I could find someone to replace me…"

Wilma's brows shot up. "The woman in the room next door is moving into Hampstead House. They tried to talk me into going there, but I told 'em I wasn't ready for that crowd. Anyway, the daughter says her mother's live-in housekeeper is going to be available and thought I might be interested. Unfortunately, the lady is allergic to cats. Besides, I'd rather have you and the girls. You're family."

Kara was touched. "Well…I guess it can't hurt to ask." She stood up. "Come on, George, let's check her out."

But as she walked beside the big dog, she had a feeling this decision was going to hurt. A lot.

BRAD SLIPPED INTO the house the way he did every night—stripping out of his black-and-white checked pants and soiled white chef's shirt in the laundry room and dumping his clothes into the hamper. Just months into their marriage, Lynette had asked him not to bring the smells of the kitchen into their bedroom. She'd been pregnant at the time and had been particularly sensitive to scents of all kinds. The habit had stuck.

He grabbed a clean, folded bath towel from the shelf above the dryer and wrapped it around his waist. He'd already kicked off his shoes in the garage, and the cold tile felt good against his hot, sweaty feet. Some nights, his shift at Willowby's felt like a marathon. Tonight was one of those nights, thanks to a dead battery on the Tahoe.

He was so used to coming home to find everyone in bed that he almost missed Kara sitting in a chair at the dining room table—sound asleep—her cheek resting flat on an inch-tall stack of papers. Her plan to franchise, he guessed.

Brad admired her drive—he'd felt the same about Willowby's once. A long, long time ago. He and Lynette and Reggie had had such big dreams when they first started out. Now, whenever Kara talked about her goals, Brad felt both envy and fear. Success would take her far away from Pine Harbor. Selfishly, he didn't want to see that happen. He liked her here. He liked his life with her in it.

She lifted her head and blinked sleepily, the way her daughters did when they first woke up in the morning. Not that he saw them every day, but lately he'd made a point to get up early on his days off so he could be part of the "family" time.

Once she had finished yawning and looked at him, she exclaimed, "Oh, wow. Nice towel. I always wondered why those were stored in the laundry room."

"Are you working on your plan?"

"Crunching numbers. Budget-wise."

He knew all about that.

The heat pump kicked in, sending a blast of cool air across his shoulders. "I'd better turn in. You staying?"

Her cheeks flushed and she looked down…guiltily. The way his son did when he had something to hide. "What do you mean?"

"Will you be staying up much longer? It's pretty late."

"Oh. Um…you're right. We should probably both be in bed. A-alone, of course. I didn't…" She jumped to her feet. "I'll shut up now."

Brad laughed. "Are you always this scattered when you wake up from a nap?"

"I didn't think I'd fall asleep. I was waiting up to talk to you."

Oh. "Oh." Another shiver passed down his back. A flash of premonition, perhaps? He had a feeling this wasn't a talk he was going to enjoy. He had options. He could hurry away, insisting he was too tired—the truth. Or he could pull her into his arms and sweet talk her into coming to bed with him—a different kind of truth. Or he could do what his ex-wife said he was incapable of and put Kara's needs before his own.

"Let me grab some sweats and a robe. I'll be right back."

Kara was sitting on the family room couch, her knees pulled to her chest, when he returned. He'd taken a few minutes to jump in the shower to wash off the scent of the restaurant and had half expected to find her snoozing again. She wasn't.

"I made us both a cup of tea," she said. "Nighttime herbal."

He sat down in the leather cigar chair opposite her. "Thanks." He took the mug in both hands and brought it close to his face, inhaling the aroma. "Nice. So, what's up? Is this about work? Are you getting ready to offer your first franchise to some savvy investor?"

"Not exactly. Staying here has given me the time I needed to figure out exactly what that would involve, and it's a lot more than I imagined. Even after Wilma comes back, I'll need another helper so I can do the legwork to scout out other locations."

He sat forward. "Do you see yourself living in another town?"

Her shrug told him yes, but she said, "Not right away."

"That's good."

"Um…Brad…"

Uh-oh. "Is something wrong?"

"I saw Wilma today."

"Oh, right. You took George. Did he behave?"

"He was a big hit. After visiting with Wilma, we toured the whole place. He seemed to love being the center of attention." She paused and studied her hands clasped tightly on the table in front of her.

Brad knew he wasn't going to like hearing what was coming. "And…?"

"Wilma's doctor is ready to release her…on the condition she has help at home. She wants me and the girls to move in."

Move? Brad didn't know what to say.

"She's been a surrogate mother to me, Brad, as well as a best friend. I owe her so much, but I told her I'd made a commitment to you and—"

Commitments. He knew all about those and how easily they were negated. Just like vows. "You don't owe me anything, Kara. Don't stay because you feel obligated."

"I can't just leave you in the lurch. Justin is doing better attitude-wise, but I still feel as though I should—"

Brad didn't let her finish. Her leaving felt too much like the last time, when Lynette told him she was sorry, but she had to go because this wasn't the life she'd imagined for herself.

"How soon?"

"You didn't let me finish. I've found a house-keeper who could take my place. A nice older woman who has impeccable references."

He stood up, suddenly too wiped out to continue. He set his mug on the end table. "That was very conscientious of you. Thanks. I'm going to bed. G'night."

"Umm…okay. I just thought you might want to call her right away. When word gets around that she's available…"

"It's two a.m., Kara. I don't think she'd appreciate it if I called tonight."

She frowned. "I didn't mean now."

"I know. You're trying to absolve your conscience. Fine. Leave her number. I'll call her in the morning."

He turned around and went to his room. Screw polite. He didn't feel the need for social niceties. Kara was leaving. Just like Lynette had. Wasn't the person getting dumped entitled to few bad manners? Pretty soon, he'd have this down to a science.

CHAPTER FOURTEEN

KARA WOKE UP the next morning with a heavy heart. Despite the sleep-inducing herbs in the tea she'd shared with Brad the night before, she'd slept poorly. The weight of her decision to move in with Wilma wasn't resting well on her shoulders.

She decided to skip church. Instead, she called her mother with the news of her decision, after which she told her daughters.

Neither of the twins was happy.

To Kara's surprise, her mother withheld judgment. "I'm sure Wilma will be very grateful. Would you like me to keep the girls today while you get started cleaning? From what you've told me, her place is pretty cluttered."

A major understatement, Kara decided an hour later. She'd been making the twice-daily drive out to the country to tend to Pooka and Dilbert, but today was the first time she entered the two-story, century-old farmhouse with the intention of actually making room for her and the girls.

"Wow," Justin exclaimed, after taking just two

steps into the home's front parlor. "What is all this stuff?"

Impulsively, she'd asked Justin if he'd like to help her—for pay. She'd told him about the move over breakfast—Brad hadn't been present—explaining that she felt an obligation to help her friend. He'd shrugged and said, "Okay." His reaction had made her worry that he'd think all women were flight risks.

Being cowardly, she'd made Justin obtain his father's permission to go with her, rather than ask Brad herself.

She hitched up the sleeves of her oldest, rattiest sweatshirt. "Wilma's a pack rat. I don't think she or her late husband ever threw away anything, and when she sold the produce business, I think she moved all the boxes here."

"Why? There's a barn outside."

Kara couldn't argue with that logic. "Excellent point. That's where we're hauling these boxes. I saw a wooden pallet leaning against the building the other day. Together we can pull it into a nice, dry stall and stack everything under a tarp."

Once they had that accomplished, she pointed out a flatbed handcart Wilma had told her about. "Bring that along."

He poked the pair of earpieces dangling on his chest into his ears and did as she'd asked. Kara had come to hate MP3 players. She and the twins had argued about the subject just a few days earlier.

"I want a music box like Justin's," Sophie had said from the backseat.

Justin, whom they'd just picked up at school, was riding shotgun, oblivious to their conversation because he had his music turned up loud enough for everyone in the car to hear.

"Maybe when you're fifty and your hearing is starting to go anyway."

"Brad said he'd buy us both one for our birthday if you said it was okay."

"He did? When was that?"

"When we went shopping."

"Well, for the record, it's not okay with me."

"But, Mommy, the earphones let you disappear. Like magic."

"Exactly. I don't want you to disappear. I love you, and I like being able to talk to you and have you hear me and answer. That's what families do. They talk to each other. Okay?"

Both girls had responded with a nice, loud "Yes." Loud enough for Justin to turn her way.

She'd planned to mention the incident to Brad, but now figured what was the point? He had his own way of parenting, and she had hers. And in a few days they wouldn't have to worry about the two methods not meshing.

"What goes first?" Justin asked, drawing her out of her reverie.

Kara looked around. "This row," she said, pointing to eight uniform, white corrugated cardboard boxes with lids stacked along the wall leading to the staircase. "I think they all contain business stuff. I'd haul the whole mess to the dump if it was mine. Some people don't know how to let go of anything."

"And some people don't know how to hang on to anything," he mumbled, his gaze dropping before she could see his eyes.

"What?"

"Nothin'." His iPod earpieces went back into place and he began loading boxes onto the dolly.

She watched him for a second. What had he meant by that? Probably that his parents hadn't tried hard enough to hold their marriage together. He didn't know about Fly, she was sure. And certainly not the fact that she hadn't begged or pleaded with him to stay after she found out she was pregnant. She'd let him go because she'd known with a certain survival instinct that she and her unborn child—children, as it turned out—would be better off without him.

She wished she could say the same thing about Brad.

She was well into her second box of nonbusiness memorabilia when Justin returned.

"Did you know there's a litter of kittens in the barn?" he asked.

"Wilma mentioned something about a stray cat roaming around, but I never spotted one. Did you see the mother?"

He shook his head. "I heard the mewing. There

are four little kittens. They don't have their eyes open, but they're making a lot of noise."

"You can show me when we take the next load out. Wanna help sort? I'm not getting through it as fast as I was because some of this stuff is fascinating and real old. It must have belonged to Wilma's in-laws. They settled in this area around the turn of the century."

They worked steadily for more than an hour, occasionally pausing to exclaim over some treasure or interesting piece of history.

"Did Wilma's husband die in some war?"

Kara eased back on her heels. "No. Why?"

He held up a dusty case containing two medals. One was a Purple Heart. The other a Bronze Star. "Wow," she exclaimed. "Is there any paperwork with them?"

Justin dug a little deeper and produced a yellowed news clipping. "Local casualty of war honored," proclaimed the headline. Kara scanned the story. "Wilma had a son. He was killed in Vietnam. She never told me."

"That's weird."

"Know what's weirder? The obituary says he was the son of Wilma and the late James Morgan. Wilma's last name is Donning. Her husband's name was Buck."

Justin's eyes grew wide with curiosity. Kara was intrigued, too—and a little hurt that her best friend had kept so much from her.

They continued sorting and repacking. Kara made

sure to separate important papers from the general junk. Sadly, the box housing the sum total of Wilma's son's life wasn't even half-full. A birth certificate, high school diploma, a few photos—bent and torn—the medals and a letter signed by the president thanking the family for their sacrifice.

"Is that all you can find?" she asked.

Justin nodded. "Not much, huh?"

"I don't get it. Her son's life barely fills one box but she's saved coupons from Mason's Drug. A store that closed up when I was a little girl." That gross disparity bothered Kara.

She had to talk to Wilma.

First, she called her mother. "Are you still at home? Good. Don't bother coming out here. Justin and I are leaving. We need to stop to see Wilma a minute then we'll swing by for the girls."

"SOMETIMES LIFE is so painful, you just want to disappear and pretend you never existed," Wilma said before Kara could even speak a word of greeting.

"I beg your pardon?"

"You found J.J.'s box, didn't you?"

Kara and Justin exchanged glances. They'd talked about what they'd discovered the whole way back to town and about whether or not Kara had any right to ask Wilma about something she'd chosen not to share with anyone. In the end, Kara had decided she would leave any revelations up to Wilma, but she still wanted to know what to do with her son's belongings.

"We found a box with an army medal," Justin said, apparently finding his voice before Kara.

Wilma was dressed in a lavender jogging suit that looked too soft and demure for her defensive posture, but a moment later the fight seemed to go out of her. "My boy," she said quietly. "His name was James Morgan, Jr."

"I didn't even know you had a son," Kara said.

"He died a long time ago. And it was my fault."

Kara was taken aback. "What do you mean? I read the article. He was a hero. He saved other people's lives. You should be proud."

"I was a fool. I met J.J.'s father the year I graduated from high school. The war was still going on, and I volunteered at an army hospital caring for wounded soldiers. Jim was the handsomest, bravest man I'd ever met. A real, live war hero. He'd lost part of his foot when he kicked a grenade out of a foxhole. Saved two other soldiers."

She sighed. "We got married while he was still on crutches. His wound got infected and it was nearly a year before they released him. By then, they'd amputated his leg up to his knee, but he was still in pain. He tried not to show it. That was the brave thing to do, right?"

She didn't wait for an answer. "He went to work for a defense contractor. We bought a house and tried to start a family. We'd almost given up when J.J. was born."

The look on her face was so tender and sad.

Kara reached out and took Wilma's hand. "You don't have to—"

Wilma shushed her. "It's time. I knew it was comin' when I sent you out there to move things around." She pulled her hand back and sat up a little straighter. "The day before J.J.'s second birthday, Jim took his own life. I didn't blame him. I half expected it. He'd lived with the pain for as long as he could stand. He made it look like an accident, but…"

Kara's eyes filled with tears.

"I moved back home to be near family. I made a life for us, and I made sure J.J. knew he'd had a father he could be proud of." She looked at Kara and said, "Pride is a double-edged sword. He was a good boy, had lots of friends, did well in school. Planned to go to college, but the day he turned eighteen he got a letter in the mail. From the draft board," she added for Justin's benefit.

She shifted in her wheelchair. "I figured he'd get a deferment—only son of a war veteran, but J.J. said he wanted to go. He needed to go—to honor his father's memory."

Wilma's face contorted in pain. "He'd listened to all those stories I told him about his father. He wanted to be just like his daddy, only I'd made Jim larger-than-life. I tried to tell him about the end of Jim's life, but J.J. wouldn't listen. He accused me of making up lies to keep him home. The last time we spoke he was angry with me. He hadn't believed me."

"Oh, Wilma, I'm sure he wasn't mad at you at the end."

"He wasn't even there six months. The chaplain who came to break the news told me he was still firing on the enemy as his helicopter went down. He was credited with saving ten other people." Wilma's lips flickered as if trying to smile. "Eight more than his father saved."

Kara walked over to her friend and took Wilma's hands. "I'm so sorry. I can't imagine what it would be like to lose a child. No wonder you never talked about it."

Wilma's thin shoulders lifted and fell. "That's not why I never told you. Truth is I was ashamed."

"Of what?" Kara cried.

"Of how I handled it. A month after I buried him, I left. Took one bag of clothes and bought a bus ticket west. I didn't tell anyone I was going. Not my sisters, or any of Jim's family. I just ran away."

"You were in shock. Post-traumatic depression."

A slight smile turned up one corner of her lined cheek. "Maybe. Mostly I wanted to disappear."

"How'd you wind up in Pine Harbor?"

"The ocean was as far as I could go," she said. "This town seemed as good as any. I got a job at JCPenney. Lived in a little apartment over the pharmacy on Main."

She reflected silently a moment then said, "I was forty-seven when I met Buck Donning. We frequented the same coffee shop every Sunday morning. I'd stopped attending church after J.J. died, but I found I missed the after-church socializing, so I'd dress up nice and go to the café. Buck never missed a mass.

"Gradually, he struck up a conversation and drew me out. As our friendship grew, I confided in him. He talked me into contacting my family. Most were gone, but one of my sisters was still alive. She's the one who sent me that box you found. She'd saved it all that time."

Kara didn't know what to say.

"Buck and I got married a month later. I never felt he judged me for what happened to J.J. or for how I ran away from my life. He was the kindest man I've ever known, and we never slept a night apart from the day we said our vows till he passed away."

Kara hugged her. "I'm glad you told me. I… um…we brought the box with us. You wouldn't like to see it, would you?"

Wilma hesitated. "You know…maybe I would."

Kara turned to ask Justin to run to the car, but he was already out the door.

"That's a good boy," Wilma said.

"You're right. He is."

"What's his father say about this move of yours?"

"He wishes us both well. And he said he'd call the housekeeper you told me about. We're fine. Everything is fine."

"Then why do you look so miserable?"

Kara was saved from having to make up a lie by Justin's return with the box. Then, it was time to go. She had children to pick up. And a man to avoid.

CHAPTER FIFTEEN

"GEORGE?" BRAD CALLED, jiggling the leash in his hand. Normally, the sound of the metal clacking would bring the big dog loping. This time nothing happened.

"Where'd he go now?"

Brad knew he was nearby because the animal had been on his heels from the time he opened the garage door a good half hour earlier.

In the past, Brad would sleep late on Sunday then spend a few hours working around the house, until it was time to open Willowby's. But since his divorce, he'd passed control of the Sunday kitchen to John. Brad was still on call, but they rarely needed him—which left plenty of hours for laundry. Unfortunately, Kara had been adding his and Justin's dirty clothes to her loads, so he had one less thing to keep him busy.

According to the note she'd left for him that morning, Kara had decided to spend the day sorting out Wilma's place. She'd hired Justin to help—and had sent Justin to him for permission instead of asking herself. The twins were spending the day with Kara's mother. That meant the house was empty and quiet. Too quiet.

Finally, unable to repress the image of her loading up her little sedan and driving away, he'd gotten up to tackle the job of cleaning the garage. George had been "helping" until he suddenly disappeared.

"George?" Brad called, rounding the side of the house. He could see a black-and-white shape moving around at the edge of the property where mowed grass met wild field. Just beyond that point was the bike path and a few yards beyond that, the cliff that dropped off to a rocky ravine where winter's runoff made its way to the ocean.

Large clumps of dirt and sod flew as the dog dug industriously. Curious, Brad jogged closer. He stopped to watch as George glanced around stealthily before using his mouth to pick up a red-and-white object from the grass. It was tubular, about eight inches long and looked vaguely familiar.

A second later, George dropped his booty in the hole then immediately started pushing loose dirt over it with his nose.

"George?"

The dog let out a little yip of panic and lay down. Brad had never seen anyone—human or dog—look more guilty. "Whatcha doing, boy?"

George wouldn't make eye contact.

Chuckling, Brad went down on one knee and brushed aside enough soil to reach the buried treasure. He pulled it out of the hole gingerly, aware that whatever it was had been carried some distance in the mouth of a dog.

A shoe. He held it by the heel and knocked the dirt from it. *Kara's shoe.* Brad remembered seeing the pair beside the back door. "Oh, George, what did you do that for? If you were going to steal shoes, you should have taken mine. Kara can't afford to go out and buy…"

He let his voice trail off. The dog didn't understand what he was saying. All George knew was that somebody he cared about—and who cared for him—was leaving.

Brad heaved a sigh, then pushed to his feet. After attaching George's leash to his collar, he hurled the shoe toward the house and said, "I'm not going to lie to you, buddy. You're right. Kara is going. As soon as Wilma gets her doctor's okay, it's just us guys again. Only this time, I'm not going to ignore you just because I feel like crap. I promise. So, how 'bout a walk?"

George didn't have to be asked twice. His powerful tail swished back and forth with joy; his jowls jiggled into a smile of sorts.

Brad was halfway to the bike path that ran along the cliff when he remembered that he hadn't left Kara a note.

"Oh, well, we won't be gone long," he murmured.

JUSTIN HELPED KARA unload the car as the twins dashed in and out of the house, talking about their baking project with Gramma Nan. Kara only half listened. Her mind was still on Wilma and the secret she'd kept for so many years.

"Do you think my mom is ever going to feel that way?" Justin asked, holding out his arms for a grocery bag. "Sorry that she just up and left like she did?"

They'd stopped at the market on the way home for one thing and had wound up with six heavy sacks. *You know better than to shop with kids,* Kara had reminded herself too late.

She clutched the bag she was carrying a little more tightly. "I think every parent has regrets about something they did or didn't do. And your mom calls you. It's not like she dropped off the face of the earth."

"Might as well have," he muttered before resuming his trek into the house.

Kara followed. She looked around, expecting to see Brad. He never left the garage door open. Even in a nice neighborhood like this, thefts occurred if you weren't vigilant.

With her elbow, she hit the power return button and hurried after Justin. This was the first time he'd really invited a dialogue about what was bothering him. Unfortunately, his timing couldn't have been worse. Kara's guilt about leaving him had been building all day. Would the new housekeeper "get" him?

"Hand me the cereal, would you?" she asked, to keep him from running off. As she rearranged boxes in the cupboard, she told him, "You were just a toddler when I worked at Willowby's. Your mother doted on you. She'd bring you to work while she did the bookkeeping, and your dad would let you help him in the kitchen." She glanced over her shoulder and grinned. "You weren't a big help, believe me."

Justin scowled, but she could see a light of humor in his eyes. "He used to make a fort for me in the storage room. It was pretty cool."

She folded the first sack and handed it to him. "I don't know what went wrong with their relationship, Justin, but you know they both still love you, right?"

"I'm never going to fall in love. It sucks."

Kara pushed the second bag away and looked at him. "That's what I said, too, when I was your age. My mother was the queen of failed relationships, and I promised myself I'd never be anything like her. So, I dated guys I knew weren't interested in marriage. My plan backfired when I got pregnant."

He grabbed a Clif Bar from the bag and ripped it open. "How come you didn't marry the twins' dad?"

"Because when I told him I was pregnant, he said, 'Sorry, babe, that's not my thing.' And he left." She shrugged. "It was probably for the best. I was too busy earning a living and being a mom to take care of him, too."

"Do the twins miss not having a dad?"

Kara paused. "I don't know. Being with just me is all they've known...well, until we moved here.

Now, they're crazy about your dad—and you. But they knew this was only temporary."

"How come?"

"How come what?"

"How come you don't stay? You and Dad are both single. You both have kids. The twins aren't *that* annoying. George likes you. A lot."

"And I like all of you. A lot. But if you're asking why your father and I aren't a couple, relationships are tricky. Sometimes, it's all a matter of timing. Now isn't a good time for me to be thinking about starting a relationship—even with someone as great as your dad."

"Why?"

She put down the sack of hot dog buns she'd been about to place in the cupboard. "Justin, you're a smart kid. You know that the term *rebound* doesn't apply just to basketball. After someone's had his heart broken or gone through a bitter divorce, it takes time before he can make intelligent, healthy decisions. I have to look out for my girls. I'm their main role model, and I have to do what I think is best for them." I can't afford to be your father's rebound fling, she didn't add.

Justin frowned, but he didn't say anything until she was done putting away the groceries. "I'm going to my room if Dad asks. Where is he, anyway?"

She scanned the countertops, expecting to see a note. "Good question. The garage door was open, but the truck is here. Is George gone, too?"

Justin walked to the window that gave him a clear view of the kennel. "The door to the dog pen is closed, but George isn't in it. Maybe they're on a walk. Can I watch the movie we rented?"

"Huh? Ummm…yeah, okay. But it isn't like your dad to take off without leaving a note. Maybe he's at the neigh—" Her thought was cut short by a loud, angry wail coming from the addition. Sadie. An even louder cry of outrage followed. Sophie. Too much sugar with Grandma.

She hurried toward her daughters' room, but she couldn't shake the feeling that something wasn't right.

CHAPTER SIXTEEN

BRAD SHIVERED ON the small rocky ledge that had saved him from certain injury, maybe even death. One minute he'd been talking on his cell phone—leaving a message on his ex-wife's parents' answering machine; the next, George—all hundred and sixty pounds of him—had jerked Brad off his feet. To keep from landing flat on his face, Brad had reared backwards several steps. His heel had slipped on the soft, unstable soil along the embankment. Teetering on the brink of falling backward, he'd clung to the leash with both hands, hoping the powerful dog would drag him back to safety.

But George must have reacted instinctively to the unusual and unexpected pressure by twisting around until he fought his way out of his collar. The next thing Brad knew the leash came flying toward his face and the sudden release of tension had provided the impetus to propel him over the edge.

The ledge he was now curled up on had broken his fall. Some adjacent tree roots had given him something to grab. His cell phone was nowhere in sight. He guessed it had disappeared into the thick vegetation below.

The irony of having made a life-changing decision one moment then facing a near-death experience the next wasn't lost on him. And if someone didn't happen by soon, he might succumb to exposure.

He curled a bit tighter to keep his core warm. Yelling for George didn't seem to be working. His calls were probably being muffled by the wind.

For now, his only option seemed to be waiting in hopes that Kara would come looking for him. Kara. The real reason he was out here. He'd spent the entire walk thinking about her, about what her moving out of his house meant to him.

"I don't want her to go, George," he'd stated out loud. "I like having her and the girls there. Justin seems less surly. I know you're happier."

George hadn't responded, but he was obviously picking up on the anxiety around him. After all, if he weren't worried about losing Kara, he wouldn't have been burying her shoe.

But unlike his dog, Brad hadn't done anything to show Kara how he really felt. Just like when Lynette asked for a divorce, Brad had stuffed everything he was feeling into a little box deep inside. He hadn't argued—except when it had come to the lot next door. He hadn't punched Reggie in the nose—even though he'd wanted to so badly his fist had ached for a week. He'd never wanted them to see how much they'd hurt him.

"Am I a coward or a fool?" he murmured. "Or both?"

A shower of gravel made him look up. A black and white snout peeked over the edge some fifteen feet above him. "George," he exclaimed, reaching up. "You came back. Good boy. You big, smart dog. Now, I need you to go get Kara. Can you do that? Go home, George. Go home."

George made a sort of whimpering sound, then his nose disappeared. Brad listened hard but couldn't hear anything beyond the roar of the wind. Dusk was starting to blur the edges of the trees. His view of the coast was blocked by trees, but he could smell the dampness of the ocean. He knew how cold it was going to get in the next few hours.

Tucking his chin into his chest and hunching his shoulders, he closed his eyes and recalled the message he'd left for Lynette—via her parents, who apparently talked to her far more often than either Brad or Justin did.

"Hi, folks, it's Brad. I'm sorry I didn't get a chance to see you when you were in Oregon, but Willowby's is keeping me busier than ever. Um, this might sound a little strange since we haven't talked in a very long time, but I need to get a message to Lynette. She called the other day and said she still doesn't have a direct phone line, so if you talk to her, would you please ask her to call me? Let her know I've decided to borrow the money from my mother to buy her share of the lot. Mom offered to help when she was here at Christmas, but, well, Lynette knows how I am about going into debt—even though I'd be borrowing against my own inheritance." He'd turned his mother down flat. Plus, at the time, he hadn't really wanted to make things easy for Lynette and Reggie.

He knew the only way he was going to prove to Kara that he was emotionally healed was by acting like a grown-up. And this was a step in that direction. Lynette was his son's mother and would always be a part of his life. The happier she was, the easier things would be for Justin.

"Also, I want you to tell her that I'll pay Justin's way to the wedding. He should be there. This is his mother—" He never got a chance to finish the thought. His words had been cut off when George lunged and his phone went flying.

Would Lynette's parents interpret his sudden yelp as a cry for help or would they assume the cell phone company had dropped his call? He didn't know. He could only pray that George would bring Kara.

KARA DIDN'T REALLY START to worry until several hours after she and the kids had arrived home. Brad wasn't answering his cell phone and nobody at Willowby's had heard from him.

"Mom, I'm telling you this isn't like Brad," she said. She was on her cell phone, staring into the shadowy dusk from the patio door. "He doesn't simply take off without telling anybody. And I promise you, unlike Tony, we will not find him at some bar watching a game."

"That was the old Tony," Nan said huffily.

Kara knew she was being unkind, but she was too upset to care. Something had happened. She could feel it. "Can you come over here right away to stay with Justin and the girls? I took them with me to walk the neighborhood, but it was getting too dark to search near the cliff. And the wind is cold."

"I know," her mother said grumpily. "I just got home from delivering cookies to Coos Bay, but at least the car is still warm. I'll be there in ten minutes."

Kara hoped they had that long. She'd called the police after she and the twins got back from talking to the neighbors but had been told a person wasn't considered missing after only a single afternoon of not checking in. "Okay. See you soon."

She sat down at the table and pulled on her galoshes.

"Anything?" she asked Justin when he walked into the kitchen. She'd put him in charge of calling every one of Willowby's employees.

"Nope. Nobody's heard from him today."

Kara's stomach fell. "I think George is the key. Where could they both be after all this time? I'm going outside to call for him again."

Justin reached for his jacket, but she stopped him with a hand on his arm. "I know you want to come along, but will you do me a big favor and stay with the twins until my mother gets here? When I get scared, they get scared. You're cool and calm. Maybe play Junior Scrabble or Jenga with them. I'll be back soon and if I don't find either your dad or George, you can help me organize a bigger search party, okay?"

"Yeah. I'll do that."

"Thank you." She gave him a swift hug. "And stay close to the phone. I'm taking my cell and that big flashlight your father keeps in the back of the truck."

"Okay."

She zipped up her raincoat, even though no rain was predicted for another day. The bright yellow material had reflective strips and it helped to block the wind. With flashlight in hand, she headed toward the bike path where she normally walked George each morning. Logic told her this is where Brad would have headed if he were walking the dog as well.

"Geo…orge," she hollered at the top of her lungs as she crossed the open field.

She panned the beam back and forth until she spotted an odd shape. She hurried over and picked up one of the red-soled walking shoes she'd set atop a box of her things in the garage earlier that morning. Looking around she discovered a fresh hole surrounded by dog prints. She knew this meant George had been here at some point.

Suddenly, an eerie sound echoed off the weathered pines and scrub bushes that were scattered along the headland. "George?" she cried, getting to her feet.

A minute later, the black and white Harlequin Great Dane burst into sight, running as if a ghost was on his tail. Kara raced toward him, calling his name. "George. Thank goodness you're okay. Where's Brad?"

She reached for George's collar but it was gone. "Oh, no, that's not good," she groaned, petting the winded dog to calm him. "Easy, boy. Slow down. Everything's going to be okay."

She stuck her hand in her pocket and felt around. Just as she'd hoped, she'd left a spare lead from the last time she'd worn the coat to bathe Prin. "Okay, George, I know you're not Rin Tin Tin or Lassie, but I need you to take me to Brad. Can you do that for me?"

She held his head and stared into his eyes, willing him to understand. After a few seconds, she kissed his nose then tugged on the leash. "Come on, George, let's find Brad."

CHAPTER SEVENTEEN

"BRAD?"

Kara called his name over and over as she followed George along the path. "Oh, where are you? Please answer me."

She flashed the light back and forth in a sweeping motion. He was out here. She knew it. Had he fallen and twisted his ankle? Maybe George had tripped him and he'd hit his head on a rock. One bad scenario after another passed through her mind as she'd searched the winding trail.

Her eyes were watering, partly from emotion and partly from the wind. She felt like she'd been walking for hours, but she knew from the clock on her phone it had only been ten minutes since she reached the trail.

George stopped to sniff something.

Brad's scent? Or scat from a wild animal? She didn't know. Knowing George, it could just be something stinky that caught his attention. George wasn't dumb, but he wasn't a trained bloodhound, either. She didn't trust him to find Brad—that was her job, but he was company. Like a walking security blanket.

George barked suddenly and pulled her toward the embankment. Kara's heart leapt in hope—until she spotted a squirrel. She yanked back. "Damn it, George, stay focused. We're looking for Brad," she shouted in frustration.

George froze, as if shocked by her reprimand. Then his great pointy ears cocked and flickered slightly. Had he heard something she'd missed or was this a clever ploy to distract her anger?

She started to pull him back to the path, but George dug in his heels and refused to budge. "Geo…orge," she said with a groan. "We don't have time—"

She tilted her head and listened hard. A faint sound tumbled on the wind. Was it a human voice?

"Brad?" She took a step closer to the edge of the cliff and cupped her hands around her mouth. "Brad," she called at the top of her lungs. "Are you there? Can you hear me?"

This time when George pulled on the leash, she followed—even though he seemed intent on leading her right to the unsafe rim. She'd learned a long time ago not to trust the crumbly soil that was undermined by wind and rain coming off the Pacific, but the sound she'd heard was growing more distinct. It was a man's voice. Brad's voice.

George stopped just shy of the edge and refused to go any farther. Kara dropped the leash then got on her hands and knees. She crawled forward until she could shine the light downward. "Brad?" she called, her voice cracking. "I'm here, Brad. Are you okay?"

"Kara? Oh, my God, George really brought you back? I can't believe it. Good dog, George."

She couldn't see him clearly. There was too much brush and roots in the way, but she realized in an instant that he was in grave danger. "Brad, I have my phone. I'm going to call for help. You have to hold on a little longer."

She couldn't make out his muffled reply and feared he might be going into shock. She didn't know if he was injured but could tell he wasn't dressed for the weather. A sweatshirt wouldn't do much to block the freezing damp wind blowing in off the ocean.

"Hang on, Brad," she repeated as her trembling fingers punched 9-1-1.

Brad lost track of time. In what could have been minutes but felt like hours before the rescue crew arrived, Kara provided a lifeline that kept him from slipping into a warm, inviting place just beyond consciousness. He heard the terror in her voice, but she kept talking. She told him about her day. About Wilma's secret and Justin's compassion. That surprised him at first, but as he thought about it, he realized he'd always known his son was a nice person. Someone who cared about others. Lynette had taught him that. She'd been the one to drag them all out of bed before dawn on Thanksgiving to cook for the homeless. How had he forgotten that?

George's frenzied barking alerted him to the fact that help had reached them. He prepared himself as best he could, but his fingers were mostly numb. Even the smallest movement hurt. Luckily, the search-and-rescue personnel who dropped over the cliff in climbing apparatuses seemed perfectly capable of extricating him from the ledge without his assistance.

He put his faith in their ropes and experience. A few tugs and he was back on solid ground. Someone wrapped a shiny blanket of some kind over his shoulders and half led, half carried him to the back of an emergency vehicle. He greedily sucked down a bottle of water once the worst of his shivers had subsided.

"Brad," a familiar voice called.

He watched her push past the young guy in uniform. The EMT backed off, obviously in deference to the dog at her side. George. His savior. Brad couldn't help but grin.

"You're smiling. That's good. You're not in pain?"

He took another drink then set the bottle aside and reached out with a shaky hand to pull her closer. "I'm a lot better now. You and George saved my life."

She let out a little peep and threw her arms around his neck. Her warm body lit a fire deep in his core. A fire that had gone out long before this experience on the ledge. He'd lost something precious—the spark he'd felt when he first got married, first opened Willowby's, first held his newborn son. Kara had brought that joy back to him. And he couldn't let her slip out of his life—the way he had let Lynette.

"We need to talk," he told her, hugging her fiercely.

She pulled back enough to look into his eyes. "We can do that once I get you home and in bed."

He wasn't sure that statement meant what he hoped it meant, but he couldn't wait to find out. Every delay—completing an accident report and arguing with the EMT about not going to the hospital—made him crazy, but finally he was able to convince them he could walk home—George and Kara on either side of him.

"I left George's leash back there," he said, stumbling slightly. His left foot was still tingly from being curled under him for so long. "I wrapped one end around myself and the other around some roots the way you did with the seat belt that first afternoon when you'd put George in your car. I figured it might be a little added security if I lost consciousness."

She emitted a small cry and squeezed his hand. "Thank God you had it. I don't even want to think what could have… I'm just glad George led me to you. You're our hero, George."

Brad let the dog have his moment. No one needed to know that George was partly to blame for sending Brad over the cliff in the first place. But reflecting on the event, Brad realized he was at fault, too, for not paying attention. He'd lost a great deal of what was most dear to him by not staying focused, and he wasn't about to let that happen again.

Kara walked back to the house with calm resolve

even though she knew she was about to make a terrible mistake. Worse than the one she made with Fly because that night she'd reacted blindly to the powerful forces of a storm that had reminded her of how much she'd lost. In her urgent haste to feel safe and loved, she'd forgotten to use protection. History, hormones and meteorology had conspired against her.

Tonight, the weather was tranquil. And she was on the pill at her doctor's advice to regulate her periods. But a hurricane of emotion was wreaking havoc inside her. She knew what was going to happen, so she didn't even try to talk herself out of it.

A few minutes after midnight—when the longest day of her life finally ended—Kara still felt the same way. She'd answered a million questions, eaten two or three bites of the pizza her mother had ordered, dutifully supervised her daughters' baths and even read them a story. But now the house was quiet, and she was ready to climb out of her skin with desire—and the very real need to physically reaffirm that Brad was alive and well.

She'd nearly lost him. He could have slipped from her life in the same flash of time that had taken her father. Uncle Kurt. Fly. Even a few of her mother's boyfriends who had lasted long enough to play a role in her life. The one thing all of the men she'd cared most about had in common was…they left.

And one way to avoid the inevitable pain that followed was to step away first—before she came to love someone too deeply. By sleeping with Brad, she risked falling in love with him. She'd been fighting her emotions for weeks and knew what she was about to do was risky, but she couldn't turn back. Sometimes even a mistake felt right at the time.

"Brad?"

She closed the door softly behind her and walked into the room she rarely entered except to drop off folded laundry. She couldn't see much of Lynette in the decor. No photos. Nothing the least bit girly.

Brad stepped out of the bathroom, wearing flannel pajama bottoms and a loosely belted robe. He was shirtless but traces of shaving cream dotted his chin and neck. He picked up a towel to rub his face then tossed it backward, not caring where it landed. "I was hoping it wasn't delirium that made me think you'd come."

His low-slung pajama bottoms and bare chest might have given him a playboy look if not for the Great Dane figures in the fabric. She had to smile. "I'm here. I probably shouldn't be," she added seriously. "We have three children just beyond that door, but…" What if this was just an overreaction, pure and simple? Was she going to feel like a complete fool in the morning?

He went to her and ran the back of his hand along her jaw. The piney scent of his shaving cream reminded her of the trees near the cliff. She gave an involuntary whimper.

He used his knuckle to lift her chin so he could

look into her eyes. "We're both single, Kara. Being together doesn't break any laws."

"I know. It's just…well, this is a big step for me. And with me moving soon, I don't want to make things more complicated than they already are."

"Then don't move."

"I have to. I promised Wilma. She needs me more than you do."

He drew her into his arms and pressed his body against hers. "I don't think that's possible," he murmured against her ear, his voice gruff with desire.

Kara stopped fighting her inner battle. If she were honest, she'd admit that she'd lost the war the day she met him. And regardless how this worked out in the end, she wasn't going to pass up an opportunity that might never come again.

He kissed her. Softly at first, as if finding his bearings, then with an abandon that erased the scribbles on the slate in her mind. Her vision went fuzzy and her knees had trouble staying locked. As if reading her dilemma, he led her to his bed so she could sit down.

A part of her wanted to believe that their driving need and intense desire stemmed from something more, something much deeper than a shared reaction to his traumatic experience. But she knew better than to give what she was feeling a name. Love.

Love had turned her mother into an emotional doormat. Love had nearly ruined her best friend's life. Love had destroyed this wonderful man's marriage. She could live without love.

But could she live without Brad?

CHAPTER EIGHTEEN

"GEORGE. SHUSH," Kara said, opening the door of Brad's bedroom. "Do you want to wake the kids?"

Kara could tell that George was confused seeing her step out of his master's room. She hadn't forgotten that he was in the house, but she *had* overslept. She'd planned to stay with Brad for a while then return to her room so she could start her day as usual.

Business as usual? Yeah, right, like that was going to be possible after spending the most amazing night of her life in Brad's bed. "I bet you need to go potty, don't you?" she asked softly, patting his head. "Come on. I'll let you out, but you have to promise to stick around. Brad will walk you later—if he dares," she added, chuckling.

He'd explained to her how the accident had happened. Just thinking about how badly he could have been injured was enough to make her queasy, so she pushed the images from her mind. She wasn't going to think about the other dark thoughts, either. Like the fact that they'd made love three times but hadn't once spoken about her impending move.

"If last night was more than just sex, he would have asked me to stay," she muttered softly. *So, obviously, I was right about him needing a rebound fling. What a surprise.*

George looked at her as if he might argue with her had he been able to talk. But Kara wasn't in the mood for any rebuttal. "Shoo. If I want relationship advice, I'll tune in to *Dr. Phil*."

She opened the door and watched George bound across the patio to the lawn, glistening with morning dew. She halfway expected him to head into the tree line, but he didn't. He stopped. Peered into the distance toward where all the action had taken place then lifted his leg on a clump of weeds. Last night had changed them all—even George.

She left him to his business and rushed to her room for a quick shower. It wouldn't be as exciting as the one she'd shared with Brad around midnight, but if she kept the water cold enough she shouldn't have to explain to her girls why she wasn't herself this morning.

Brad heard the sound of water running in the addition. He stretched. And groaned. A couple of muscles weren't ready to let him forget that he'd been curled up on a ledge for a few hours. But the pain was offset by the memory of spending the night with Kara.

She'd tried to slip away around four to return to her bed, but he'd coaxed her—seduced her, actually—into staying. They'd made love three times and discovered they fit together as if they'd been made for each other. The happiness he felt made his chest feel as if it might burst. The only problem was her upcoming move.

He'd planned to sit her down this morning and lay out a rational argument for why she should stay with him rather than cart her family off to a hundred-year-old farmhouse. But was that smart? he asked himself.

They'd agreed this was a one-time thing. Neither of them wanted to send the wrong message to their children. Could he really be expected to share a house with Kara and not want her?

After last night? Impossible.

And then there was the matter of his unintentional declaration of love after the first time they made love.

She'd immediately gone still. Drawing back enough to face him in the silvery moonlight spilling in from the curtains he'd forgotten to close, she'd kindly attributed his words to "post-traumatic shock," then went on to explain that such bursts of emotional largesse were common in people who had survived a near-death experience.

"I don't really love you?"

"You nearly died. As a result of that, you love life. And at the moment, I'm a part of your life. That doesn't mean what you feel is the real thing."

"It's real. See?" he'd said, placing her hand on his very animated penis. "Love. Lust. Gratitude to be alive and in bed with you. Yep, it's all real. Trust me."

She'd giggled and reacted as he'd hoped she would—with the uninhibited passion that had dazzled him from their first kiss. But her blithe dismissal of his declaration had hurt, and he hadn't brought up the subject of her staying for fear it would fall under the same category.

Hopefully this morning, in the clear light of day, they could talk like adults. He stretched and inhaled deeply.

The faint scent of coffee made him hop out of bed. His left knee buckled. He quickly dropped back to the mattress so he didn't wind up on the floor and rubbed the muscles of his thigh and calf.

"Knock, knock."

He looked over his shoulder to find Kara approaching with a cup in hand. "'Morning. I was just getting up, but my knee isn't cooperating."

Her bottom lip popped out the way it did when she was comforting her daughters when they suffered a boo-boo. "Maybe you should see the doctor today. The EMT guy wasn't very pleased when you refused to go to the hospital."

He took the mug she handed him and breathed in the fragrance of the brew. "Thanks. This is all I need."

"My uncle was just as ornery about taking care of himself. He might have had a few more years with us if he'd seen a doctor sooner."

"I liked your uncle. He used to bring his lady friends into the restaurant. Friendly. Funny. A real character. I bet you miss him a lot."

She nodded. "I do. What hurts most is that the twins will never know him. Or their grandfather."

He reached for her, intending to give her a hug of comfort, but she backed away from his hand. "I…um…last night was…um…we didn't really talk about what would happen today, but I think we'd better go back to the way we were. Justin might figure out what happened, but the girls won't. And I'd rather keep it that way."

"You would?"

"Yes. We're leaving soon, and I don't want Sophie and Sadie to get the wrong impression. They have fairy tale-itus, as it is. You're the handsome prince. I'm the tragic princess. If they found out we were together—even though they don't know what that consists of—they'd assume that meant we were getting married and going to live happily ever after."

Married. The word nearly made his coffee make a return trip up from his stomach. He couldn't speak because he was too busy trying not to be sick. Being in love was one thing. Setting himself up for another failure at something he obviously was really bad at was another.

"Brad," Kara said, compassionate as ever, "it's okay. After what you've been through, you might never want to get married again. I understand. But I can't live with you and have an affair. That's not the role model I want to be for my daughters."

She stepped closer and touched his cheek. "Last night was a wonderful gift that I'll always treasure, but today we move on with our lives."

His fingers gripped the mug so tightly he half

expected it to break apart. How could she be so cool and composed when he couldn't even find his voice? Mute. Just as he'd been when Lynette broke the news that she was leaving him.

And wasn't that what Kara was doing? Leaving?

She paused by the door. "Justin's school is doing conferences and testing today. If you're not feeling up to it, I could try to reschedule."

"I'm not an invalid," he snapped.

She reacted to his tone with a little wince, but a second later, her shoulders righted and she said, calmly, "The girls and I are leaving now to feed Wilma's cats. See you later, I guess."

Then she was gone.

He slumped forward. Anger was quickly replaced by something he couldn't even identify. Hopelessness? Helplessness? Inertia?

"Dad?"

He glanced up. "Huh?"

"Kara said you're taking me to school. Do you want me to put George in his pen?"

The dog in question plunged into the room, barreling straight into Brad's midsection. George's bony crown smacked him in the chest—right above his aching heart.

He grabbed the dog's head squarely between his hands and looked into the animal's funny, mismatched eyes.

George went still. He stared back without blinking.

"From now on, George goes with us."

"Really? Cool. You like to ride in the car, don't you, boy?"

George's tail swished back and forth. He squirmed slightly and Brad let go to pet his neck and shoulder.

"That's not the only change I want to make around here," he said, turning to his son. "You and I are going to talk more."

"Do we have to?"

Brad couldn't tell if he was being sarcastic or not. "Yes. As I was curled up on that ledge, thinking I might not make it back, I realized that somehow I'd become my father. He was a good man. Hardworking, but distant. If I wanted to tell him something, I went through my mother. Like she was some kind of interpreter. I don't know how or why that happened, but I think it's safe to say you were a lot closer to your mother than to me before she left. Right?"

Justin nodded.

"And, at some level, I'm sure you blame me for what happened. And you'd be right. I think I pushed your mother away. I was too wrapped up in work and didn't see that she needed more than I was giving her."

Justin looked at George as if shocked by Brad's admission. "Um. She wasn't happy, Dad. Not for a really long time. You might not have been able to fix that, but I do think you let her go too easily."

"I should have fought Reggie for her?" Brad asked, only half joking.

His son shrugged. "You didn't seem to care when she told you she wanted to be with him."

"I cared, but my ego got in the way. And then I found out about the money. I was hurt and mad. But I want you to know that I'm sorry I didn't fight harder to make our marriage work. I should have listened better. I'm going to listen better now."

"To me?"

"Yes. And to George."

That made Justin smile. George cocked his head in his goofy, inquisitive way at the mention of his name.

"What about Kara?"

Brad sighed. "Good question. It doesn't sound like she's going to be around much longer to listen to, does it?"

"Then make her stay. That house that she's moving to…smells like cats. And there's all this stuff around. Sophie and Sadie won't like it there. And…" He paused as if searching for the right words. "I don't want them to go. They're a pain in the butt, but they're okay some of the time."

Brad was too surprised to speak. Instead, he got up and limped to where his son was standing. He pulled him into a quick hug. "You're a pretty smart kid. Maybe you learned from your mother's and my mistakes. With your help maybe I won't screw things up too badly this time."

Justin returned the hug—for a couple of seconds. Brad let him go. He put his hands on his hips and let out a long sigh. "So, where do we start? Do I ask her to marry us?"

Justin rolled his eyes. "You're so lame. Even a guy my age knows you start by talking to her best friend."

Brad started to laugh. His chuckle grew to a guffaw. Through his tears he could see the amused look his son and George exchanged. They thought he was crazy. And he was. Crazy in love. And for the first time in a long time, he felt a flicker of optimism. Kara hadn't said the words, but surely she felt the same way he did.

He was positive she did. But she was also afraid. And Justin was right. When a girl was undecided, it helped to have her best friend on your side.

He wiped his eyes and started toward the bathroom, favoring his left leg slightly. "I'll head over to Wilma's as soon as I'm through at your school, but we have a couple of other errands to do first. Number one, we need to replace my cell. I was leaving a message on your grandparents' answering machine when I fell. My phone went flying."

"Why'd you call Grandma and Grandpa?"

"I figured they'd talk to your mom before we did. I told them to tell her you would be at the wedding. No ifs or buts. Now, go start the truck."

As he hurried into the shower, he was still smiling at the look of surprise on his son's face. And there'd been another emotion there, too. Hope.

KARA PLODDED UP the sidewalk to Wilma's front door. She was trying to focus on how to make the approach easier on a woman using a walker. Short of pouring new concrete and building a ramp, she didn't see how the access could be improved enough to make a difference.

Sadie squeezed her hand. "Are we going to be late for school?"

Sophie, who usually spoke first, looked around Kara and answered, "Mommy hates to be late. She doesn't like it when the teacher scolds her. Right, Mommy?"

The worrier and the pragmatist.

Kara sighed. "You won't be late. This will only take a minute, as long as you don't let the cats out."

"But what about the kittens in the barn?" Sophie asked. "Justin said there are babies and no mommy around."

Thanks, Justin. "He didn't see the mother cat, but I'm sure she was just hiding because he was a stranger. If we leave them alone, they'll be alright."

"Where's the daddy?" Sadie asked.

"Gone," Sophie answered sagely. "Like ours. Like Mommy's, too."

Kara's heart, still fragile from leaving Brad the way she had, cracked open, threatening to send her into tears. Sophie's matter-of-fact tone of acceptance seemed to say that this was how life was, so why fret about it? Was that the lesson she'd unintentionally taught her daughters? To believe that fathers never stuck around?

She led the twins to the front step and sat down,

pulling them into her arms. "Listen, girls, I need to make something clear. Your father is a really nice guy. We had a lot of fun together when he lived here, but he wasn't ready to settle down and be part of a family. If I'd tried to make him stay, nobody would have been happy. But not all dads are that way. Mine wasn't. He was a wonderful man and he would have been an awesome grandfather."

"Why'd he leave?" Sadie asked.

"He didn't. He died. I told you the story. He was trying to help some people during a bad storm."

"The river swept him out to sea and he drowned," Sophie stated as if by rote.

"Pretty much. My point is you can't judge all men by what happened to me. Brad is a dad, and he's here for Justin."

"An' us," Sadie put in.

"Nu-uh," her twin countered. "We're moving, remember?"

Huge crystalline tears welled up in Sadie's eyes. "But I don't wanna go. I like living with Justin and his daddy. I want Brad to be my daddy, too."

"Well, he can't be," Sophie stated emphatically.

"Why not?" Sadie wailed.

Sophie's look of scorn turned pensive. After a moment, she said, "Because the prince always kisses the princess and he hasn't kissed Mommy. Has he, Mommy?"

Kara's cheeks heated. "You know, we have to hurry or you'll be late for school. I really do hate it when your teacher gives me that look. So, let's go. We have cats to feed and things to learn and dogs to wash."

She didn't usually avoid answering her daughters' questions, but, in this case, she honestly didn't know what to say. Yes, Brad had kissed her and made her feel things she didn't want to feel. But he hadn't asked her to marry him. Or even asked her to stay, for that matter.

And why should he? she asked herself as she helped the twins fill the cats' dishes. His heart is still mending. And while his divorce might be legal, he and Lynette still hadn't settled the division of property. Why would a man who wanted to be free of a woman throw up roadblocks to keep her from disappearing out of sight? Obviously, Brad wasn't ready to let go of what he and Lynette had shared. A woman would have to be a needy, codependent fool to get involved with a man who was still attached to his ex-wife.

And while Kara might be a little impetuous during storms and after evenings of high emotional turmoil, she wasn't her mother.

CHAPTER NINETEEN

"WHAT AM I DOING?" Brad said aloud.

He'd left the junior high a few minutes earlier and was headed in the direction of the rehab center where Wilma was staying on the advice of his teenage son—a kid who hadn't even started dating.

"This doesn't feel right. I barely know the woman. Why would she help me when it's in her best interests to have Kara move in with her?" he pondered aloud. Glancing in the rearview mirror, he saw George watching him over the far rear seat. "This is crazy, isn't it, boy?"

George woofed.

They were parallel to the city park, which offered a three-block buffer between Brad and the hospital complex where the center was located. He pulled over, got out, went to the back of the truck and opened the rear door.

"How 'bout a quick run in the park while I think about this?"

The big dog barreled out of the opening. Brad caught him by the collar—an old one that Justin had found in the garage, along with a frayed but service-able leash. "Sorry, boy. There's a leash law in this area, but, at least, there aren't any cliffs for you to pull me over."

The dog walked sedately at his side for two blocks, and then, as if getting his bearings, veered right. "Whoa, George, hang on a minute. I haven't made up my mind yet about talking to Wilma."

George strained at the leash, determined to head in the direction of a one-story brick building sur-rounded by neatly groomed green lawns and flower beds. The rehabilitation clinic. George had been there with Kara. He'd probably enjoyed all the atten-tion and wanted to go back, but Brad wasn't ready.

Spotting a park bench a few feet away, he pulled George over to it. "Give me a minute, George. I've already done a lot this morning, and I need to catch my breath."

Not literally, but he had accomplished a lot in a short time. First, he and Justin had driven to Willow-by's. Next, they'd headed to the mobile phone store, arriving just as the manager opened its doors. Natu-rally, the process had taken longer than he'd ex-pected so they'd had to race to school to make Justin's conference. Brad had been pleased to learn that his son had settled down, both socially and aca-demically. His midterm grades had improved in all subjects and he'd expressed an interest in going out for sports again—something that would only be possible if Brad could convince Kara to stay.

Brad had had two reasons for making the cell phone store a priority. Symbolically, the phone was important because it meant he was available to his son any time of the day. But that communication went both ways, so he also purchased Justin a phone and had it programmed with the numbers from his old phone—the one they'd retrieved from his desk at Willowby's. Giving it to him after his positive progress report seemed all the more fitting.

"There are a lot of names you can delete, but the numbers for your uncles and aunts should still be good," he'd explained. "And as soon as your mother gets a land line, you can add hers, too. Just remember, there's a four-hour time difference between here and the Yucatán, and you're earning your minutes by working for me."

Justin had seemed impressed with the sleek new model. "Cool. Can I download some other ring tones online?"

"I guess so. And I want you to add a couple of other numbers. Kara's and The Paws Spa."

"Why do I need Kara's if she isn't staying with us?"

"Well, because of George. Another thing that crossed my mind while I was on the ledge was something your counselor told me. She said kids your age need to feel they're making a contribution to the family. She suggested giving you more responsibility. So, if Kara moves out, I thought I'd put you in charge of George. Grooming appointments. Rabies shots. Boosters. Whatever he needs."

"But Kara does that so well," Justin had replied, laying it on so thick Brad had nearly groaned. "She needs to feel included, too, right? Talk to Kara, Dad. Please. Convince her to stay—for George's sake."

Brad now looked at the dog in question. George was staring at the rehab center as if it held a year's supply of dog food. His snow-white chest glistened from the tender grooming he'd been receiving.

The dog turned to Brad.

"You're a good dog, George. And almost as smart as my kid, but what happens next is important. Kara is loyal to the max. She might not like it if we talk to Wilma behind her back."

Brad studied the building where Kara's best friend was staying. "So I'm going to talk to Kara instead. This is between us." He stood up and started back toward the car but was abruptly halted when the leash went taut. "George. Come on. Let's go."

George stubbornly pulled in the opposite direction.

"George," Brad said sharply.

George's tail stopped wagging.

Brad stepped closer to release the tension in the leash. "George. Sit." The dog obeyed with obvious reluctance. Brad met his eyes. The blue one seemed alight with excitement, the brown wise and encouraging.

"I told myself last night that I was going to start listening to the people around me. That includes you. You want to see Wilma? Fine. We'll talk to Wilma. But if Kara gets mad about this, it's your fault. Got it?" Brad said aloud, realizing too late that several elderly patients out for a stroll were standing a few feet away.

He nodded hastily and hurried toward the building. He didn't know if he needed special permission to bring George indoors with him but hoped that since the dog had visited a few days earlier he would be welcome today as well. George led the way straight to Wilma's room.

Fortunately, the lady in question was awake and sitting in her wheelchair by the window. George barked a hello. Wilma startled as if deep in thought, and turned to look at them. "'Bout time you got here," she said, staring right at Brad. "I was beginning to wonder if you even deserved her."

"Pardon?"

Wilma shook her head. "Men. No offense, George." She motioned for the dog to come closer. To Brad, she said, "Sit down. Heard you had a little excitement last night."

He assumed she meant his fall, but his mind immediately flashed to an excitement of a different kind… with Kara. To hide his blush, he took his time pulling up a chair. "Did Kara tell you what happened?"

Wilma rubbed the skin around George's neck in a way that made him moan with pleasure.

"Nope. My friend, Margaret, called. Her daughter drives the school bus. She heard about it from a student whose father is an EMT. Some are speculating you might have jumped on purpose."

Brad put his face in his hands and cursed under his breath. "For the record, I'm not suicidal. I lost my balance—with a little help from George."

The dog's ears shot upward at his name. He cocked his head at Brad. "Not that it was George's fault. I was on the phone and I wasn't paying attention. Seems to be a chronic problem in my life. One I'd like to change."

"Sounds like a good idea."

"I think so, and according to my son, I've done better since Kara has been living with us."

"Why do you think that is?"

Brad swallowed. "Because I love her."

"Does she know that?"

Brad felt the heat return to his face. "I told her how I felt and she said that was my near-death experience talking."

Wilma's loud bark of laughter made George bark as well. Brad was so embarrassed the tips of his ears were burning. "Sounds like Kara. The girl isn't prone to whims of the heart like falling in love. She looks long and hard before she leaps."

"How do I convince her this isn't a whim?"

"Why are you asking me?"

"Because you're her best friend, and according to Justin, best friends know things other people don't."

Wilma didn't refute that. "So, what's your plan?"

Brad tensed. He'd been thinking about how to proceed all morning. "Well, I'd like to convince her to stay. Everything feels right with her there. The

girls are happy, and Justin's doing great, but after…
um…last night, I think Kara and I both know we
can't just live together. So, I thought I'd go to The
Paws Spa and ask her to marry me," he said bluntly.

Wilma and George exchanged a look that made
Brad's stomach clench. "Won't work. She's got it in
her head that she has to move to the farm and take
care of me. I could hire someone, but you know
Kara. Loyal to the max."

Brad agreed. "Okay. So, she moves in with you
until you're better. That would give us time to plan
a wedding." *And go out on a date.* "What are we
talking? A month? Two?"

Wilma frowned. "My doctor said I'll never be
able to live alone again. I've got osteoporosis. Weak
bones," she clarified. Her thick white brows knitted
together. "And a couple of other old-age health
issues I don't want to talk about."

Brad tried to think of something kind and sup-
portive to say, but the only word echoing in his
brain was *never?*

The sudden, intrusive sound of a siren filled
the room. George leapt to his feet, hackles raised.
Brad leaned over to grab the dog's leash. "It's
okay, boy," he said, gently soothing the animal.
"Relax. Sit. Good dog."

Nobody spoke for a minute or so, then Wilma
cleared her throat and told him, "I always say you can
tell a lot about a person by the way he interacts with
animals. You have potential, Brad Ralston. Wasn't

sure about that when George kept running away from home every chance he got, but I'd be willing to bet you have a dog biscuit or two in your pocket, don't you?"

Oh, nuts. I didn't know there was going to be a test. He stuck his hand in the pocket of his Dockers. He didn't remember grabbing any treats that morning, but as he wiggled his fingers, he touched something that definitely wasn't a key or money.

George moved closer, sniffing with interest.

Brad produced the doggie bone, triumphantly. George, obviously assuming the biscuit was for him, snatched it from Brad's fingers and devoured it in one bite.

Brad started to protest, but George looked so happy, he didn't have the heart to scold him. Instead he said, "You're a good dog, George, but next time wait for my cue."

George pushed his head squarely against Brad's chest, leaving Brad no choice but to hug him and Wilma, no choice but to smile. Brad liked the way it softened her face, making her appear more grandmotherly.

A silence lingered, then she asked him, "How do you feel about cats?"

Brad had never owned a cat in his life and really didn't care to. He was about to admit that, but George butted him in the chest again, and when he looked into the dog's eyes, he knew to change his answer.

"I love cats," he lied.

BY THE TIME Kara picked up a brush to finish grooming Banjo, her last client of the afternoon, she was about ready to jump off the same cliff Brad had tumbled over the night before. The morning had flown by, but Claudia had returned from lunch certain she had food poisoning. After throwing up twice, she went home, leaving Kara alone to handle four dogs.

Normally, this wouldn't have been a problem, but Kara had been counting on Claudia's nonstop chatter to keep her brain preoccupied. And since none of her clients were very talkative, that left Kara with far too much time for introspection.

And what she'd concluded after all this thinking was she'd made a terrible mistake. She'd chosen Wilma over Brad. Not really, of course, but that was how he'd see it. And after his ex-wife's defection, how could he not be devastated by Kara's decision?

She wanted to call him and explain the rationale behind her choice but knew he was without a cell phone at the moment. She didn't dare leave a message on the home answering machine in case Justin heard it.

"Helloooo," a voice called just as the bell over the door of The Paws Spa jingled. "Anybody here?"

"Mom?" Kara said, nearly dropping the brush in her hand. "What are you doing? Why aren't you at work?"

Nan walked in, set her purse on Kara's desk and hurried to the raised table where Kara was working. "I got off early. In fact, I have the whole week off. I have fabulous news and I wanted you to be the first to know."

Kara's mostly empty stomach did a crazy flip-flop. "What?"

"I got a promotion. 'Bout time, don't you think?"

Kara was shocked. Her mother had complained through the years about her lack of mobility within the phone company, but Kara had assumed this was mostly due to Nan's lack of initiative.

She put down her brush and gave her mother a hug. "Mom, that's great. What will you be doing?"

"Oh, mostly the same thing I am now, but I'll have people under me. They offered me the job a few years back, but I didn't think I could leave you and the girls at the time. Now that you've got a man to take care of you, I can do this without feeling guilty."

"I beg your pardon?"

"Brad. I've seen how much happier you are since you moved in with him. Not always worrying about every penny and how you're going to get ahead."

"Mother, I'm staying at his house, not *living* with him. There's nothing roman—" She couldn't say the word. She wasn't a liar.

Nan didn't seem to notice. "Oh, you know what I mean. Besides, it's only a matter of time before you two do connect. I felt the vibes last night. Unmistakable."

Kara hadn't been herself last night. She'd been reacting with her heart, not thinking with her head. "The man had just fallen off a cliff. He could have died. Of course I was a bit emotional. That doesn't mean…" She wanted to deny what had happened after her mother left the house, but the words got stuck in her throat.

"You slept with him," her mother exclaimed so loudly, Banjo nearly skittered off the table.

Kara soothed the animal, hoping to mask the fact that her cheeks were on fire. "I…"

Nan grabbed her hand. "Honey, it's okay. Brad's a good man. You deserve someone like him in your life. What's the problem?"

Kara couldn't answer, at first. She helped Banjo off the grooming table and walked him to the holding pen. His owner would be here any minute. Kara didn't want the high-strung dog picking up her inner turbulence.

Once she was safely out of earshot, she said, "The problem, Mother, is I don't want to give my heart to a guy who is still in love with his ex-wife. You married Doug when you were still in love with Dad, and remember how that turned out? He took his resentment out on me."

Nan's expression changed. "Oh, honey, how could I ever forget? I made so many mistakes in my life, but there isn't one I regret more than that. I should have listened to my instincts, but at the time I was afraid that I couldn't make a life for you on my own."

She appeared so sad, Kara couldn't stay mad.

"I left him as soon as the insurance money came in. I'd planned to use your father's life insurance to set up a scholarship for you. But, after just a few months with Doug, I realized this was your dad's way of protecting you."

The memory of the day she and her mother left Minneapolis came into her mind. Shortly after Doug had left for work one morning, she and her mother walked to a used car dealer, bought a small Ford wagon, loaded up their belongings and never looked back.

For some reason, Kara had forgotten about her mother's bravery. Why had she always chosen to believe that her mother's decisions had revolved around the current man in her life, not her daughter?

Nan sat on the corner of Kara's desk. Her business-casual slacks and white blouse made her look younger and more vibrant than Kara could quite grasp.

"I know what you're thinking, Kara. That I've made a mess of my life and I'm stuck in a rut with my loser boyfriend, but, honey, Tony isn't like the others. He's done so well in rehab—all of his therapists are convinced he's going to make it this time. Tony says that's partly because of me. I'm the first person who's ever stood by him and made him believe he could be more than just a good-for-nothing drunk."

It hit Kara that her mother had a talent for supporting other people's dreams—evidenced by how much she'd encouraged Kara over the years.

"I honestly think he's going to pull this off. And moving out of Pine Harbor will help."

"You're moving?"

"That's part of my promotion. I have to work out of the main office in Coos Bay. I could commute, but you know how much I hate driving in the rain."

"You're moving?" Kara repeated.

"I sold the trailer this morning. You'd be surprised by how much property values have gone up—even for a three-bedroom piece of junk on a leased lot." She laughed lightly. "Tony and I are going to rent at first, but we plan to buy a place together once he's working."

Kara wished she could share her mother's optimism about the man's ability to stay clean and sober, but maybe Nan was right. Maybe a fresh start would work wonders. "I'm really happy for you, Mom, but the girls and I are going to be lost without you."

Nan made a negating gesture. "How is that possible when you're so happy living with Brad?"

Brad. How like her mother to pin Kara's happiness to a man. "Mom, I'm moving to Wilma's in the next week or two, depending on how long it takes the contractor to make the place handicap accessible. Brad and I are housemates. Our arrangement was mutually beneficial, but once I leave, I'm sure he'll find a housekeeper to replace me. He never even blinked when I told him my plans."

"Well, I think you're wrong about that. And even if you didn't intend it, moving to Wilma's could be a brilliant tactical maneuver on your part."

"What does that mean?"

"Honey, sometimes men don't know what they

have until it's gone. Brad's going to wake up one morning and realize his life sucks without you in it. He'll be at that old farmhouse inside a week, begging you to come back."

"Mom, I don't need Brad to—"

Nan made a yadda-yadda gesture. "Kara, wake up and smell the…dog shampoo." She grabbed the handiest bottle and shook it at her. "You are an amazing woman. You've built a successful business out of nothing more than an old Laundromat and a dream. You're a great mother, raising two little girls alone. No one will ever take that away from you, but give yourself a break. It's okay to love somebody and be loved in return."

"But…"

"But nothing. Did I pick poorly a couple of times? Yes. But I also chose your dad. Didn't I?"

The truth hit Kara like a shower from a wet dog. "Y-yes."

Her mother smiled with satisfaction. "The mistakes came later, and I learned from them all. I know you don't think much of Tony, but give me a little credit. If he falls off the wagon, I'm kicking his butt to the curb, as they say. And if that happens, I promise to take my time and look carefully before crossing that street again." She made an X above her heart.

Kara gave her mother a big hug. A crazy mix of emotions rushed through her, but she didn't have time to examine any of them closely because Patti Metz arrived a minute later to pick up Banjo. The boxer started barking raucously, and Nan covered her ears. "And I thought my customers were noisy complainers."

Kara smiled.

Her mother was halfway to the door when she apparently changed her mind and returned to where Kara was standing. "I have an idea. The rest of this week is going to be really hectic, but I could take the girls tonight. They can help me pack, and I've been planning to let them pick out whatever of my stuff they'd like to keep—for dress-up. I held off because you didn't have much space at your old house, but if you move into Brad's place permanently you will."

"Mom," Kara scolded. "I told you. I'm moving to Wilma's. And her house is overflowing with junk."

"Another reason not to leave Brad's. Why don't the twins sleep at my place tonight so you and Brad can have some alone time." Nan frowned. "Well, except for Justin, but what the heck? He could come, too."

Kara was touched, but she shook her head. "That's sweet of you to offer, but Justin usually has a ton of homework. The twins, however, would be thrilled and *I* could really use the time to pack. Sophie and Sadie try to help, but their hearts aren't in it."

"I can't imagine why. Leaving a gorgeous home to move into a cluttered old farmhouse…."

Kara smiled at her mother's relentlessness. "Stop. They're adventurous girls like their grandma. They'll love the farm."

Nan rolled her eyes. "Do you or don't you want me to pick up the girls from Esmeralda's?"

Kara looked at the clock. "I do. That would be great. I'm supposed to meet a remodeling contractor at Wilma's in an hour, and afterwards I'll need to stop by the rehab center to tell Wilma what he said."

Nan was clearly not appeased, but she kept any further doubts about Kara's plan to herself. Instead, she hugged her. "Call me later, but let it ring. The twins and I are going to be up to our elbows in boxes."

Kara watched her mother leave, before hurrying across the room to where Patti stood. "Sorry about the wait," Kara said, ringing up the bill. "I trimmed Banjo's nails a little shorter like you asked, but you should keep an eye on them and make sure he doesn't overdo it for a day or two. We both know how rambunctious he can get."

Patti wrote out a check and placed it on the counter. "I will. Thanks. I…um…Kara…I've been meaning to talk to you, but you're always so busy. Do you have a minute?"

Not really. "Sure. What's up?"

"Tell me if I'm out of line, but I heard a rumor that you might be selling this place, and if you are, I'd be interested." Before Kara could reply, Patti added, "I've been with the bank for over half my life and there's a new merger in the works. To eliminate some of the higher salaries, they're offering me a golden parachute. One that would give me some working capital to invest in a new career. I've been bringing Banjo here for two years now, and I've been watching all your changes with interest. I really think you're on the right track by appealing to a high-end, boutique market."

"You do?"

"Yes. Plus, I've always loved animals. After a lifetime of working with people, I think this would be a very welcome change."

Kara smiled. "Well, I have to warn you, all of my clients come with owners—and they aren't all as pleasant as you've been." They both laughed. "But seriously, The Paws Spa isn't for sale. Who told you that?"

"Wilma, actually. We're in the same bridge group. She said you were looking to expand. Maybe I misunderstood. I figured if you were opening a second place, this one might be available."

"Oh, I see. Yes, a slight misunderstanding. I'm considering offering franchises. Same name, group buying power. I figured they'd be in different towns, but it hadn't occurred to me to sell this place."

Patti seemed disappointed. "Oh. My mistake. Unfortunately, I can't leave Pine Harbor. Aging parent issues. If you ever change your mind, please let me know, okay?"

Leave Pine Harbor? Leave Brad?

"Sure. I'll think about it."

"Great. I'm familiar with business trends, Kara,

and you've tapped into a major growth market. People love their animals, and we want the best for the ones we love, right?"

Kara nodded, but for reasons she couldn't quite define, the woman's words seemed to bore a hole straight through her heart.

CHAPTER TWENTY

KARA WAS EXHAUSTED, physically and emotionally, by the time she reached the rehab center. Her conversation with Patti had provided a sense of validation—and some intriguing possibilities—but the extra time had made her late to meet with the contractor who was giving her a bid on Wilma's house.

The man had been cordial and helpful, but he'd also spelled out in no uncertain terms that he couldn't start any structural work until the vast majority of boxes and clutter had been cleared away. To make the place handicap friendly, he'd need to build a ramp, widen doors and install grab bars in the main floor bathroom. His estimate of what the job would cost sounded reasonable to Kara, but his schedule was booked solid for six weeks.

What am I going to do with Wilma for six weeks? she wondered.

She trudged inside, gagging slightly from the smell of precooked food. She hadn't eaten much all day, and her latte from the drive-thru Starbucks wasn't settling well.

Wilma was sitting up in bed with a mobile tray table in front of her. The plastic plate offered a slice of overdone roast beef covered in thick brown gravy, a mound of mixed vegetables—from a can—and an anemic-looking salad. "Hey," she said. "That looks good."

Wilma burst out laughing. "You're a terrible liar."

Kara collapsed in the wheelchair and kicked out her feet on the end of the bed. "You're right. I should have asked, 'Does it taste better than it looks?'"

Wilma used her fork to stab a hunk of meat. "Not really," she said, chewing. "But I gotta keep up my strength so I can get out of this place."

Kara tilted her head back and gazed at the ceiling. "Yeah, well, about that…I've got good news and bad news. Which do you want first?"

"Neither. I'll tell you my news, instead."

Kara sat up. "But I just spent an hour with a strange man at your house. Well, he wasn't strange, but you know what I mean. He was pretty nice, actually. He's faxing me a bid tomorrow, but he can't do the work for a month or longer." She paused. "That's the bad news."

Wilma chewed and swallowed. "Okay. Now, do you want to hear my news?"

Kara frowned. This was Wilma's future they were talking about. What could possibly have happened that was more important? "Okay."

"I've got a line on a one-story, handicap accessible apartment that includes meals and would take my cats."

Kara's mouth dropped open. "You're kidding. I thought you didn't want to go to Hampstead House."

"I don't. This is a private arrangement."

"It sounds perfect. Tell me more."

"I can't."

"Why not?"

"My landlord-to-be has to move his current tenant out. He's working on it."

Kara groaned. "Oh, please, don't tell me this is Morris Jakes. You can't believe a word he says."

Wilma shook her head. "It's not Morris. After what you went through, I wouldn't rent a litter box from him. I should know more tomorrow."

Kara studied her friend's face. Wilma wasn't telling her something. "Are you okay? The doctor's still happy with the way your hip is healing?"

Wilma made an impatient gesture with her fork. "I'm fine. There's a storm coming is all. You're not the only one who doesn't like lightning and thunder."

Kara looked toward the window. "It just started to sprinkle as I drove up."

"Good thing Brad didn't fall off the cliff tonight. He might not have been able to hold on till you found him."

Kara frowned. She'd talked to Wilma earlier but hadn't mentioned Brad's accident. "How'd you…?"

"Margaret's daughter heard the story from one of the paramedics' kids."

"Oh. Well, yes, it was a close call. Fortunately Brad wasn't hurt and everything is fine. Is Margaret the one who offered you an apartment?"

"She lives with her daughter. Where are the twins?" Wilma asked, changing the subject.

"At Mom's. She got a promotion and will be moving to Coos Bay next week. The girls are helping her pack."

"Well, isn't that interesting? Good for Nan. Seems like a lot of changes going on all at once around here."

"Tell me about it. This afternoon, Patti Metz talked to me about buying The Paws Spa. She said you gave her the idea."

Wilma shrugged. "I might have mentioned something about your dream of setting up franchises."

Kara returned to the bed. "Wilma, she doesn't want to open a new one. She wants *this* place. That would mean the girls and I would have to move and open a new shop in another town."

Wilma frowned. "Oh."

"I know. I love it here. This is my home. You're here. And…and…Brad and Justin."

Wilma took a big breath and pushed her tray away. "What are you going to do?"

"I have no idea. The girls would be heartbroken. They're not even happy about moving to your place. Sophie told me on the way to school that she likes to visit the farm but she doesn't feel right about leaving Justin and Brad. Sadie agreed, although she did say she wouldn't mind bringing the baby kitties back here to live with us."

Wilma smiled. "I love those girls. You've raised them to know what they want and to go after it."

"But what if what you think you want isn't what's best for you?"

"Could you say that again? In English."

Kara sat down on the bed beside Wilma's feet. "I'm so confused. The twins aren't the only ones who have enjoyed living at Brad's... But my goal in life—my dream—has always been to be a strong, self-reliant role model for my daughters. I can't give that up just to stay with Brad—even if he did want me, which I'm not convinced he does."

She took a deep breath and slowly let it out. "You're my best friend. You know me better than anyone. What should I do?"

Wilma didn't say anything but her frown intensified. "I can't make that decision for you, Kara. But I can tell you from experience that the most important thing you can do is listen to your heart. After my son died, I didn't want to care about anyone or anything ever again. I shut people out. I thought I could live alone the rest of my days, but I was wrong. We need love in our lives, Kara. It's what makes us whole."

Kara agreed, but what if the timing of that love was all wrong?

She left a short while later with a promise to call Wilma the next morning to find out if she had any news about her mysterious apartment. The rain had intensified during her visit, and by the time she was half a mile from Brad's house her windshield wipers were on full speed—keeping time to the beat of her heart.

When her cell phone rang, she pulled over to answer it, afraid to take her eyes off the wet, slippery road.

"Hello?"

"Where are you? You're usually home by now."

Brad. He sounded worried.

"My meeting with the contractor ran a little long. I'm at Adams and Western, and it's pouring. Do you need something?"

"Yes." There was a long pause. "You."

Kara's hands trembled and her throat closed. The back and forth whish of the windshield wipers combined with the steady drone of the rain made her feel isolated. Vulnerable. But this time the storm inside could prove to be far more turbulent than any wind or hail.

"Are the girls with you?"

She swallowed. "N-no. They're spending the night with my mother."

"Really? That's interesting. Justin's next door, studying with a friend. He won't be home until nine. That gives us plenty of time."

"Time to what?"

"Eat. I fixed us a little something. Are you hungry?"

Famished. Suddenly, she felt as empty as a bottle in her recycling bin—and only one man could fill her up.

BRAD STOOD BY the back door and watched Kara's car turn into his driveway. She usually left her small sedan outside. He hadn't invited her to use the stall left available when Lynette drove away and never returned. Kara had never asked to park inside. In fact, it just now occurred to him to question why the subject had never come up.

As the beams from her headlights reached the building, he pushed the wall-mounted button. The garage door lifted. He could read her confusion even through the downpour. He walked into the middle of the empty stall and motioned her forward, miming the actions of the person guiding a jet to its hangar.

The car inched ahead.

Once it was completely inside, he made a slicing motion across his neck and smiled, but she didn't turn off the engine so he walked to the driver's side. "You're safe and dry. You can get out now."

She turned away as if to pick up her purse, but not before Brad saw the sparkle of tears on her cheeks. Such a simple thing, but it obviously meant something to Kara. Maybe she'd been right. Maybe he had been holding on to the life he'd had with Lynette in ways he hadn't even realized.

He reached down and opened the door. "It's really coming down. Let's get you inside where it's warm. Are you okay?"

She nodded, but she didn't look okay. She was beautiful, but he could read the tension in her posture. "You need a glass of pinot noir. I just opened my favorite. It's one I found on a trip to the Edna Valley in southern California."

She handed him what appeared to be a bundle of mail and a new collar and leash. The price tag showed The Paws Spa logo. "George hates his old collar," she said by way of explanation.

"He told you that?" Brad said, smiling.

"Pretty much. You have to read between the lines with George. He's a male, you know."

Brad was still chuckling as they walked into the kitchen. Kara stopped dead in her tracks and tilted her head back. "Oh, my Lord, what is that fabulous smell?"

"Herbed pork loin with roasted garlic and Yukon gold potatoes and mixed greens. Pumpkin soup. And pear tart with chocolate hazelnut sauce."

She closed her eyes and inhaled again. "Wow."

He put his hand on the small of her back and gently prodded her forward so he could put down his load. "And on the side, we have French fries and hot dogs for the girls. Justin ate before he went next door."

She pivoted to look at him. "That was so nice of you. Sophie and Sadie love your fries."

He reached past her to pick up a DVD. "I also rented them a movie so we could have some alone time," he said, nodding toward the dining room where he'd set an elegant table complete with crystal stemware, the good silver and flowers.

Her hand went to her heart. "Oh, my. How beautiful. It looks like something out of a magazine."

"It's supposed to be romantic."

"Why? When I left this morning... Well, I wouldn't blame you if you just wanted me out of here as soon as possible."

He shook his head. "That isn't going to happen."

"But—"

He leaned in and kissed her to stop her questions. Just a quick, tender promise of more to come. "Later. First, you need to unwind." He helped her out of her raincoat and then handed her the stemless wineglass that he'd filled after talking to her on the phone. "This will help."

She examined the glass a moment before taking a sip. "Oooh, yummy. I'm no connoisseur, but it tastes lovely. Are these new glasses?"

"Glad you like it. Yes. I only bought two. Follow me. You'll see why."

She walked beside him past the family room where George was stretched out in front of the fireplace. The dog lifted his head and made a small snort of greeting but didn't get up.

"Did you drug him?" she asked, her tone telling him she was teasing. "He usually rushes to greet me."

"I worked him. We did a lot of shopping today and...a few other things."

"Hmmm," she murmured through another sip of wine. "Where are you taking me?"

He opened the door to his room but didn't turn on the light. He didn't want her to see all the changes he'd made just yet, but the glow of light from the master bathroom gave them a clear path to follow. "It smells good in here, too. Lavender?"

He led the way to the bath so she could see the oversize oval tub surrounded by tea candles in sparkling little globes. The mirrors and windows were all steamed over and a huge mound of bubbles glistened like scattered diamonds.

Her gasp of surprise pleased him. He hadn't needed anyone to tell him that Kara's life hadn't been filled with decadence and pleasure. She worked hard and rarely gave herself permission to relax and enjoy the rewards of that hard work.

"For me? Now? But you have dinner cooking. I should—"

He took the wineglass from her hand and set it on the wide rim of the tub. "I bought that glass specifically for this moment. See? Nice and stable. Less likely to tip over and break. All you have to do is relax in the tub. Trust me, I'm a seasoned chef. I know all about timing. The meal will be ready when you are."

She didn't seem to take in what he was asking, so he turned her to face him and put his hands on the top button of her Paws Spa cotton shirt. His fingers smelled of garlic, but they adroitly worked downward.

He expected her to stop him at some point, but she didn't. She lifted her arms to facilitate the removal of her T-shirt. She wiggled her hips to help him yank down her jeans, and she stepped out of her panties when he pulled them to her ankles. Within seconds she was naked. And obviously chilled. Her nipples were a ruddy pink and rigid. Her breasts, while full and lush, were not the perky perfection they probably had been before she nursed her twin daughters.

"You are so beautiful," he said, wanting desperately to skip the bath, dinner and everything he had planned. He crushed her to him and kissed her until he felt her melt against him.

He knew she wouldn't have objected to any change in plans, but he marshaled his self-control and moved back slightly. "As much as I'd like to join you in that tub, I have greens to sauté. So, you hop in, unwind and meet me in the dining room when you're ready." He glanced at the clock on the counter. "Will twenty minutes do the trick?"

She looked at the tub. "I usually feel selfish if I take a six-minute shower."

He took her hand as she stepped over the edge and slowly inched into the hot water. Once she was settled back against the blow-up headrest he'd picked up on one of his stops, he handed her her glass. "I left one of your warm-up suits on the hamper. I took it from the pile of clean clothes in the laundry room so I didn't have to dig through your things."

With eyes closed and a small, satisfied smile on her lips, she barely acknowledged his comment. Brad grinned and quietly slipped out of the room. He stopped long enough to look at what he'd accomplished that afternoon. The room-darkening drapes were gone. He planned to make some changes in his life, even if Kara chose not to be part of it. No more late nights at work. He had a crew in place that could easily provide the same high quality that had earned Willowby's its reputation. He would still oversee the menu, the purchasing and the personnel; he'd make the soups and desserts and his signature sauces. Then, he'd come home to be with his family. Hopefully, a family that included Kara, her daughters, Justin and any other children God saw fit to give them.

As he hurried past the family room and spotted his dog sprawled on his back, legs splayed outward like a giant dead bug, he laughed out loud. "And you, of course."

George's ear twitched but his eyes didn't open.

Standing at the Viking stove Lynette had insisted they needed, he added an inch of wine to his glass then paused a moment before turning on the burner. Lynette's vision of their marriage had never matched his, he realized. In theory, he could appreciate the idea of nightly meals cooked on this lovely, high-end appliance. In reality, the only cooking he'd ever done in this kitchen was for holidays and guests.

But that was then.

This was now.

And the new life he had in mind also included an eighty-something woman and her cats. *Am I crazy?* a part of him wondered.

No. Just in love, a voice in his soul answered. And when Kara joined him, all relaxed and receptive from her soak, he planned to ask her to marry him.

CHAPTER TWENTY-ONE

KARA DIDN'T NEED a clock to tell her when to leave her wet, fragrant cocoon. The water was starting to get cool and the pads on her fingers and toes were looking a little withered.

She polished off the last of her wine, blew out all the candles and stood up. She held the big, fluffy plum-colored towel that she'd probably washed and folded but never had used before to her nose and inhaled deeply. Fabric softener, but also a trace of Brad.

She dried off and dressed quickly. The luxurious respite had been just the break she needed to recoup her equanimity. So much had happened in such a short time. What would Brad say when she told him about Patti's offer?

She swallowed a sigh and hurried toward the kitchen. George appeared to be snoring peacefully; otherwise, she would have given him his new collar and leash.

"Um…hi. What's a girl gotta do to get a refill around here?"

Brad was standing at the stove with his back to her, stirring something in a big stainless-steel pot. He whipped around, automatically cupping his palm to catch any drips. "Ouch," he said, blowing on his palm. "Hot soup."

He made an adjustment to the flame and wiped his hand off before walking to her. "Wow. You look…revived."

She passed him her glass. "I am. What a luxury! I've never been in such a big tub. And the candles made me feel so pampered."

When he rinsed it under the faucet, Kara was a little disappointed. The wine had tasted so good, but he was probably right not to give her more. She needed to keep her wits about her. She had a lot to tell him.

After checking on the dishes in the oven, he walked to her. Leaning in close, he inhaled. "Um, you smell good. Did you like the lotion I picked?"

She grinned. "I thought that scent was a little girly for you. You bought it for me?"

He nodded. "The clerk at the bath shop where I got the headrest asked me what your favorite scent was. I didn't know, so I told her anything but wet dog."

Kara laughed, surprised to discover he'd gone to such trouble for her. "Whatever it is—" she pushed back her sleeve and sniffed her arm "—I love it."

"Freesia and clover."

"Nice."

He smiled. "Let's sit down at the table. Everything is ready, and you know from your days at Willowby's how testy the chef gets when his food goes out cold."

He helped her into her chair and pushed it in. His gallant manners made her remember the first time she ate at a fancier chain restaurant with Fly. She'd worn a skirt and heels to impress him. He hadn't seemed to notice. He'd sat down without even glancing her way as the maître d' had pulled out the chair for her.

"Cloth napkins and the good china. I'm impressed."

"The dishes were my mother's. You haven't met her, have you?"

"No."

"I didn't think so, but she was here over the holidays for nearly three weeks. I thought she might have taken George for one of his appointments during that time."

No. George had been mostly AWOL from The Paws Spa until he started coming on his own. She didn't say so. She just admired the exquisite table setting. Gerber daisies—her favorite—were arranged in a cut-glass vase. The centerpiece was set to the side so when Brad joined her it wouldn't block their line of vision.

He quickly, efficiently delivered two bowls of creamy soup garnished with a swirl of sour cream and a sprig of fresh parsley. "There's warm bread in the basket. I hope you're hungry."

"Mmm," she moaned on an exhale. "This smells wonderful."

He sat down, poured them each wine from a new bottle. Before drinking, he held his glass up to toast. "To the future—yours…mine…and ours."

Kara's hand was shaking as she lifted the elegant crystal goblet to her lips. "Brad…"

"Eat, my love. Having worked for me, you no doubt remember how particular I am about presentation. Reggie used to say all chefs are frustrated artists at heart."

She remembered. And knowing how much of himself he'd put into this effort touched her deeply. She ate with gusto, exclaiming over the hint of toasted anise seed in the soup. Later, when he served the main course, her senses were dazzled by the subtle combination of rosemary and green peppercorns seasoning the meat and the tangy compliment of the salad. The dessert tart was a perfect finish—light yet scrumptious.

"Brad, you've outdone yourself," Kara exclaimed, inching her plate to one side. "I don't think I can eat another bite. That was fabulous. Amazing. Unbelievable."

"Good. I'm glad you liked it because you know what they say, 'The way to a woman's heart is through her taste buds.'"

"Who says that?"

"I believe it was Wilma. This was her idea."

"It was?"

"George and I dropped by to see her earlier. Didn't she tell you?"

Kara shook her head. "She said she had an offer for a new apartment..." Her brain needed only a few seconds to make the connection. "You're the mysterious landlord? You offered her a place to live?"

"Not exactly. That was her idea, too. But a brilliant one. I'm sure I would have thought of it eventually," he added with a wink. "As you know, the addition is handicap accessible."

"But if you move Wilma in, where are the girls and I supposed to go?"

He took a deep breath. "A few doors down the hall. This is a three-bedroom house, remember?"

She tried to picture herself sharing a room with Sophie and Sadie. After the few days they did that when her rental house was without a roof, she'd sworn never to subject any of them to that lack of privacy again if she could avoid it. "I don't think that would work."

He jumped to his feet and grabbed her hand. "Come on. Let me show you."

They stopped in front of the closed door directly across the hall from Justin's room. He looked a bit embarrassed as he said, "This is just a start. I'm not a decorator and I didn't have a lot of time, but you can get the idea."

He opened the door and flipped on the light switch. Kara stepped over the threshold. Gone was the desk, computer that she'd never seen turned on and exercise machine that had served as a catchall. Instead, her daughters' white bunk beds sat against the wall, neatly made. The abundance of pink visible through the partly open closet door told her he'd moved all of their clothes, too. Frida the turtle's terrarium sat atop Brad's old desk.

"Where—?"

"Most of my junk is in a Willowby's van. The woman I hired to take Claudia's place is getting married next month and she said she'd take anything that I wanted to get rid of."

Kara swallowed the lump in her throat. "And my stuff?"

He made a wiggling motion with his finger. The short walk down the hall to the master bedroom left her breathless—with anticipation. He flipped on the overhead light switch. She'd been so wiped out earlier she hadn't even noticed her surroundings. Now, all she could do was stare.

The heavy room-darkening curtains were gone. The walls were bare. Even the masculine bedspread was missing. The room was a blank palate—except for the little touches that were hers.

She walked to the side of the bed she'd slept on the night before and touched her Betty Boop alarm clock. She'd had the thing since she was Justin's age and it had survived every move. Beside it sat a framed photo of the twins.

He coughed to draw her attention to the walk-in closet. The boxes of personal belongings that she'd stored in the garage were neatly stacked below her hanging clothes.

"You shouldn't have, Brad. I told you this morning. I can't sleep in your bed. It would give the wrong message to the children—yours and mine."

She meant to sound stern but could tell by his smile that she hadn't succeeded. "I know. I agree. That's why we have to get married. As soon as possible. We definitely don't want to set a bad example for the kids."

Kara's eyes filled with tears. "Married?"

He walked to the highboy dresser and opened the top drawer. "I have this on loan. The jeweler is a friend of mine, and he said we could come in tomorrow and exchange it for something you like better." Then, just like in the movies—and her dreams—he dropped to one knee and handed her the tiny box.

"You're kidding. This is for real? You want to marry me? Me? A single mother with twins?" She swallowed the huge lump in her throat.

"A soon-to-be married mother of twins and step-mom of a teenage son," he corrected. "Kara, I know you're worried about whether or not I'm over Lynette, and all I can say is when I found out she was getting married, I was jealous—that it wasn't you and me. The property settlement is done. I took care of the last of that this afternoon. Lynette's free to move on with her life, and I'm ready to do the same."

She looked into his eyes and knew he was telling the truth. This wasn't a desperate, impulsive rebound choice. The only urgency came from their situation—and a core need that she felt, too.

"If you say yes," he prompted. "But first, you have to open the box."

She tried, but her hands were shaking too badly. Brad chuckled softly and helped by covering them with his own. Together they pried apart the spring-loaded jaws.

Kara saw something sparkly. She knew it was a diamond but other than that, all she could see through her tears was a blur. It slipped too easily over her finger, but she clenched her fist tightly to keep it in place then threw her arms around his neck. "Brad. I can't believe this."

"You haven't said yes yet."

She swallowed and licked her lips. "I had another offer today."

"Of marriage?"

She smiled. "No. A business proposition. One of my clients heard I was thinking of franchising. She loves The Paws Spa and liked the idea of being part of a chain. The only problem is she can't leave Pine Harbor."

"So if you wanted to open a second shop, you'd have to sell her this place and move somewhere else?"

"Uh-huh. Probably Coos Bay or Ashland."

He sat back. "Wow. Your dream on a plate."

She nodded.

"What are you going to do?"

"I'm not sure—about that offer. I have to think

about it, long and hard. But this one…" She held up her hand to reconfirm there was a glittering diamond on her ring finger. "That's a given." She grinned. "I love you, Brad. Yes, I'll marry you."

He looked stunned. "Really?"

She kissed him as her answer. She poured every ounce of the love she felt into her silent "yes" and when she came up for air, he was smiling. "Do I need to call the twins and ask permission to marry their mother?"

"Actually, Sophie and Sadie told me this morning they want you to be their daddy. My only fear is that this will confirm in their minds that fairy tales are real." She frowned. "I'm not sure that's a good thing, but at the moment I'm too happy to care."

He hugged her fiercely. "What about your mother?"

Kara couldn't help but giggle. "Trust me. She'll be delighted. Her greatest fear was that I'd never find a man to take care of me."

Brad laughed. "You're kidding, right? You don't *need* me in your life, Kara, but even my dog knows how much I need you."

He leaned in to kiss her, but she stopped him. "Speaking of George, I think he should be the first to hear the good news, don't you?"

Brad was powerless to resist the sparkling humor in her eyes, but he knew she was serious. Besides, given the fact that Justin was due home soon, they couldn't consummate their engagement the way he'd prefer.

"Good idea. And I think it's only fair he celebrates with some perfectly seasoned pork loin."

Kara laughed and together they ran down the hall. George made a grunting sound and rolled over when they entered the family room. They were within a few steps of him when his nose started twitching.

Blinking in obvious befuddlement, the big dog slowly stretched and sat up. He glanced from Brad to Kara and back. Brad wasn't sure if he was asking "What's up?" or trying to determine which of them had the food he smelled.

George went to Kara first. She petted him effusively and removed his old collar. "I brought you a present, my friend. Red is so your color, and the silver studs are macho plus," she said, attaching the new collar around George's neck. "Perfect for a heroic rescue dog."

George stretched his jaw upward as if modeling his new neckwear, and then he turned to Brad, big nose crinkling with interest. Brad was holding a plate behind his back. "Yes, I have a treat for you, George. But first, Kara and I want to tell you that you never have to run away again. She's going to be your mother now."

"And you know what that means, George," Kara added after kissing him on the nose. "Free grooming for life."

George's eyes widened, then he smiled. Well, maybe the smile was just Brad's imagination, but George truly did look happy. Brad added to the dog's joy by offering the treat he'd been holding behind his back.

George polished off the serving of pork with three vacuum-like bites.

"What about Justin?" Kara asked after Brad set the plate on the nearby end table. "Are you sure he's going to be okay with this?"

Brad pulled her into his arms. "He'll definitely be thrilled about not having to take care of George full-time. As for our news, we can either call him on his new cell phone or wait to tell him when he comes home."

He watched her mentally juggling their options. Was she thinking the same thing he was? If Justin tarried a little longer at his friend's house…

"Text message?" they said in unison.

Laughing, they sat together on the love seat and composed a short note as George watched. "Kara = yes. Marry soon. OK U?"

He pushed the send key, and was about to pull Kara back into his arms when George got between them, sniffing their hands. He licked Kara's ring then placed his head on her lap. He startled seconds later when Brad's phone beeped, alerting them of a text reply.

Brad held the small screen so Kara could read his son's answer. The word *cool* was followed by a smiley face. Next, he'd written: "hmwrk dun. movie on. 9:30 OK?"

Brad glanced at his watch. It wasn't quite eight. "Should we let him stay out a little later?"

Kara leaned in to him, grinning. "Well…his homework is done—even if his spelling is atrocious. And an extra half an hour…"

Brad had no problem filling in the blank. Unfortunately, his thumbs felt the size of basketballs as he punched in "make it 10." Then he tossed the phone over his shoulder and pulled Kara to her feet.

As they turned to leave, she paused to look at the dog sitting nearby. "Thanks, George. You truly are my hero."

"George?" Brad said, faking indignation. "What about me?"

She touched his cheek with her hand. "You're the love of my life, but none of this might have happened if your dog hadn't run away from home."

Brad chuckled softly and nodded at the Great Dane who was watching them intently. "She's right, George. We owe you big-time. Organic dog bones for life, my friend."

George's brows shot upward and his jowls curled back in a doggie smile, then he lowered himself to the carpet and stretched out, with a long, rumbling sigh that seemed to say, "Finally. Finally, life is good again."

* * * * *

Welcome to cowboy country...

Turn the page for a sneak preview of
TEXAS BABY
by
Kathleen O'Brien.
An exciting new title from
Harlequin Superromance for everyone
who loves stories about the West.

Harlequin Superromance—
Where life and love weave together in
emotional and unforgettable ways.

CHAPTER ONE

CHASE TRANSFERRED his gaze to the road and identified a foreign spot on the horizon. A car. Almost half a mile away, where the straight, tree-lined drive met the public road. He could tell it was coming too fast, but judging the speed of a vehicle moving straight toward you was tricky.

It wasn't until it was about two hundred yards away that he realized the driver must be drunk…or crazy. Or both.

The guy was going maybe sixty. On a private drive, out here in ranch country, where kids or horses or tractors or stupid chickens might come darting out any minute, that was criminal. Chase straightened from his comfortable slouch and waved his hands.

"Slow down, you fool," he called out. He took the porch steps quickly and began walking fast down the driveway.

The car veered oddly, from one lane to another, then up onto the slight rise of the thick green spring grass. It just barely missed the fence.

"Slow down, damn it!"

He couldn't see the driver, and he didn't recognize this automobile. It was small and old, and couldn't have cost much even when it was new. It was probably white, but now it needed either a wash or a new paint job or both.

"Damn it, what's wrong with you?"

At the last minute, he had to jump away, because the idiot behind the wheel clearly wasn't going to turn to avoid a collision. He couldn't believe it. The car kept coming, finally slowing a little, but it was too late.

Still going about thirty miles an hour, it slammed into the large, white-brick pillar that marked the front boundaries of the house. The pillar wasn't going to give an inch, so the car had to. The front end folded up like a paper fan.

It seemed to take forever for the car to settle, as if the trauma happened in slow motion, reverberating from the front to the back of the car in ripples of destruction. The front windshield suddenly seemed to ice over with lethal bits of glassy frost. Then the side windows exploded.

The front driver's door wrenched open, as if the car wanted to expel its contents. Metal buckled hideously. Small pieces, like hubcaps and mirrors, skipped and ricocheted insanely across the oyster-shell driveway.

Finally, everything was still. Into the silence, a plume of steam shot up like a geyser, smelling of rust and heat. Its snake-like hiss almost smothered the low, agonized moan of the driver.

Chase's anger had disappeared. He didn't feel

anything but a dull sense of disbelief. Things like this didn't happen in real life. Not in his life. Maybe the sun had actually put him to sleep….

But he was already kneeling beside the car. The driver was a woman. The frosty glass-ice of the windshield was dotted with small flecks of blood. She must have hit it with her head, because just below her hairline a red liquid was seeping out. He touched it. He tried to wipe it away before it reached her eyebrow, though, of course that made no sense at all. Her eyes were shut.

Was she conscious? Did he dare move her? Her dress was covered in glass, and the metal of the car was sticking out lethally in all the wrong places.

Then he remembered, with an intense relief, that every good medical man in the county was here, just behind the house, drinking his champagne. He found his phone and paged Trent.

The woman moaned again.

Alive, then. Thank God for that.

He saw Trent coming toward him, starting out at a lope, but quickly switching to a full run.

"Get Dr. Marchant," Chase called. "Don't bother with 911."

Trent didn't take long to assess the situation. A fraction of a second, and he began pulling out his cell phone and running toward the house.

The yelling seemed to have roused the woman. She opened her eyes. They were blue and clouded with pain and confusion.

"Chase," she said.

His breath stalled. His head pulled back. "What?"

Her only answer was another moan, and he wondered if he had imagined the word. He reached around her and put his arm behind her shoulders. She was tiny. Probably petite by nature, but surely way too thin. He could feel her shoulder blades pushing against her skin, as fragile as the wishbone in a turkey.

She seemed to have passed out, so he put his other arm under her knees and lifted her out. He tried to avoid the jagged metal, but her skirt caught on a piece and the tearing sound seemed to wake her again.

"No," she said. "Please."

"I'm just trying to help," he said. "It's going to be all right."

She seemed profoundly distressed. She wriggled in his arms, and she was so weak, like a broken bird. It made him feel too big and brutish. And intrusive. As if touching her this way, his bare hands against the warm skin behind her knees, were somehow a transgression.

He wished he could be more delicate. But he smelled gasoline, and he knew it wasn't safe to leave her here.

Finally he heard the sound of voices, as guests began to run around the side of the house, alerted by Trent. Dr. Marchant was at the front, racing toward them as if he were forty instead of seventy. Susannah was right behind him, her green dress floating around her trim legs.

"Please," the woman in his arms murmured again. She looked at him, the expression in her blue eyes lost and bewildered. He wondered if she might be on drugs. Hitting her head on the windshield might account for this unfocused, glazed look, but it couldn't explain the crazy driving.

"Please, put me down. Susannah... The wedding..."

Chase's arms tightened instinctively, and he froze in his tracks. She whimpered, and he realized he might be hurting her. "Say that again?"

"The wedding. I have to stop it."

* * * * *

Be sure to look for TEXAS BABY,
available September 11, 2007,
as well as other fantastic Superromance
titles available in September.

HARLEQUIN® *Super Romance*®

Welcome to Cowboy Country...

TEXAS BABY

by *Kathleen O'Brien*

#1441

Chase Clayton doesn't know what to think.
A beautiful stranger has just crashed his
engagement party, demanding that he not
marry because she's pregnant with his baby.
But the kicker is—he's never seen her before.

Look for TEXAS BABY and other fantastic
Superromance titles on sale September 2007.

Available wherever books are sold.

HARLEQUIN® *Super Romance*®

**Where life and love weave together
in emotional and unforgettable ways.**

REQUEST YOUR FREE BOOKS!
2 FREE NOVELS PLUS 2 FREE GIFTS!

HARLEQUIN®

Super Romance®

Exciting, emotional, unexpected!

YES! Please send me 2 FREE Harlequin Superromance® novels and my 2 FREE gifts. After receiving them, if I don't wish to receive any more books, I can return the shipping statement marked "cancel." If I don't cancel, I will receive 6 brand-new novels every month and be billed just $4.69 per book in the U.S., or $5.24 per book in Canada, plus 25¢ shipping and handling per book and applicable taxes, if any*. That's a savings of close to 15% off the cover price! I understand that accepting the 2 free books and gifts places me under no obligation to buy anything. I can always return a shipment and cancel at any time. Even if I never buy another book from Harlequin, the two free books and gifts are mine to keep forever.

135 HDN EEX7   336 HDN EEYK

Name _____ (PLEASE PRINT)

Address _____ Apt. _____

City _____ State/Prov. _____ Zip/Postal Code _____

Signature (if under 18, a parent or guardian must sign)

Mail to the **Harlequin Reader Service®:**
IN U.S.A.: P.O. Box 1867, Buffalo, NY 14240-1867
IN CANADA: P.O. Box 609, Fort Erie, Ontario L2A 5X3

Not valid to current Harlequin Superromance subscribers.

Want to try two free books from another line?
Call 1-800-873-8635 or visit www.morefreebooks.com.

* Terms and prices subject to change without notice. NY residents add applicable sales tax. Canadian residents will be charged applicable provincial taxes and GST. This offer is limited to one order per household. All orders subject to approval. Credit or debit balances in a customer's account(s) may be offset by any other outstanding balance owed by or to the customer. Please allow 4 to 6 weeks for delivery.

Your Privacy: Harlequin is committed to protecting your privacy. Our Privacy Policy is available online at www.eHarlequin.com or upon request from the Reader Service. From time to time we make our lists of customers available to reputable firms who may have a product or service of interest to you. If you would prefer we not share your name and address, please check here. ☐

HSR07

The latest novel in The Lakeshore Chronicles
by *New York Times* bestselling author

SUSAN WIGGS

From the award-winning author of *Summer at Willow Lake*
comes an unforgettable story of a woman's emotional journey
from the heartache of the past to hope for the future.

With her daughter grown and flown, Nina Romano is ready to
embark on a new adventure. She's waited a long time for dating,
travel and chasing dreams. But just as she's beginning to enjoy
being on her own, she finds herself falling for Greg Bellamy,
owner of the charming Inn at Willow Lake and a single father
with two kids of his own.

DOCKSIDE

"The perfect summer read." —Debbie Macomber

*Available the first week of August 2007
wherever paperbacks are sold!*